The Hardy Boys
in
The Outlaw's Silve

The Hardy Boys® Mystery Stories

The Outlaw's Silver

Franklin W. Dixon

Illustrated by Leslie Morrill

Armada

First published in the U.S.A. in 1981 by Wanderers Books,
A Simon & Schuster Division of Gulf & Western Corporation.
First published in the U.K. in 1982 by
Angus & Robertson (U.K.) Ltd, London.
First published in Armada in 1983 by
Fontana Paperbacks, 8 Grafton Street, London W1.

Printed in Great Britain by
The Anchor Press Ltd, Tiptree,
Colchester, Essex

Contents

1 *The Devil Doll*

"Boy, this heat is really getting to me!" Chet Morton declared. "I need a banana split in the worst way!"

Joe Hardy laughed. "It seems to me your mother packed you an adequate lunch."

"How could she pack a banana split? Listen, I've been slaving all morning, burning up energy, and those sandwiches were just not enough to stoke up sufficient body fuel."

"I guess not," lanky Biff Hooper teased. "After all, you've got plenty of storage capacity."

The boys had been unloading bricks at a construction site for Tony Prito's father and had worked up hearty appetites. Even though they had brought sandwiches, they were looking forward to dessert at a downtown ice-cream parlor.

"Let's get a booth," said Frank Hardy and added, "Hey, watch it!" as someone jostled him roughly just before they reached the little restaurant.

Dark-haired and eighteen, Frank tended to be calmer and more even-tempered than his younger brother Joe. But his good-looking face flushed with anger as he slapped away a hand groping in his jacket pocket.

"What's the matter?" Tony Prito asked.

"Pickpocket!" Frank exclaimed, turning to scowl at the person who had just passed him. He had caught only a fleeting glimpse of a tall man with beetling brows and a drooping black mustache, but he was ready to chase after the culprit if anything had been stolen.

Quickly, Frank reached in his pocket to feel for the familiar shape of his wallet, but his hand closed on an object pressed against the soft leather. Instead of taking something, the alleged pickpocket had left behind a memento!

In the ice-cream parlor, Frank took out the object to inspect it more closely. It was a weird little plastic figure, resembling a kangaroo with bat wings and a spear-pointed devil's tail.

"What's that?" Chet Morton inquired.

"Search me." Frank frowned as he studied the tiny devil doll. "That guy I thought was a thief must've stuck it in my pocket!"

"Oh, oh, here we go again!" Biff grinned. "Another mystery for the Hardy Boys!"

"Maybe that's why he put it in your pocket," Tony suggested, then broke off as the waitress began serving their orders.

"What do you mean?" Frank asked, after she had left.

"Well, there could be some mysterious curse attached to the thing—it sure *looks* devilish enough!"

"You can say *that* again!" Chet muttered between mouthfuls of ice cream.

"Anyhow, say he recognized you as one of those famous young detectives, Frank and Joe Hardy. So he planted the devil doll in your pocket, hoping you'd unravel the curse." Tony sounded half joking, half serious.

Frank smiled wryly. "Aw, knock it off."

"If you ask me, he might just be right," said Biff.

Joe Hardy nudged his brother's arm. "Get a load of that flat-nosed guy in the corner booth."

Frank put the devil doll on the table in front of him and glanced over at the tough-looking man Joe had referred to. He was thickset with short, bristly

9

hair and the twisted, broken nose of a boxer who had stopped a straight punch. He was eyeing the Hardys and the weird figure intently.

"Big eyes and big ears," Joe muttered.

Suddenly, the man seemed to realize he had been noticed. He averted his gaze and busied himself with his food. A minute or two later he snatched up his check and walked hastily to the cashier's counter.

The place was overflowing with noontime business. Amid the comings and goings of customers, the Hardys soon forgot the flat-nosed busybody.

Suddenly, there was a muted crash of breaking glass somewhere at the rear of the ice-cream parlor.

"What in the world was that?" Biff exclaimed.

"Either someone dropped some glassware or broke a window," Tony guessed.

Moments later, smoke began to billow out of the kitchen.

"Great!" said Tony sarcastically. "Now it looks like someone started a fire!"

As the smoke increased, patrons began to cough and mutter anxiously. Some called out to the counterman and waitresses nervously, trying to figure out what to do. Suddenly a voice shouted, *"Fire!"* and the stampede was on.

Chairs scraped as people jumped up from their tables to head for the door. There was angry jostling as other customers squirmed out of their booths to join in the exit rush.

"Come on!" Frank said to his friends. "Let's try to help evacuate people. This could be a disaster if we don't!"

Calling out loudly to the patrons, the boys worked their way through the crowd.

"Please form a line to prevent injuries!" Frank commanded. "There will be plenty of time for everyone to get out as long as you don't create delays at the door. Please stay in line and walk quickly without pushing the people ahead of you!"

He was gesturing to a group of women in the back of the room while Joe and the others had worked their way toward the exit, trying to keep people calm. Frank's clear voice had a soothing effect on the frightened patrons, and they did their best to cooperate.

The din subsided a bit and the ice-cream parlor gradually emptied. When there were only a few people left, the boys went toward the door. Biff and Tony held the bandannas they had been wearing around their necks to their noses as makeshift smoke filters. The others could only keep their heads down, pinch their nostrils, and grope blindly through the fumes.

By the time Frank neared the door, the smoke was so thick it was almost impossible to see. Sud-

denly he was hit on the head from behind! The blow was only glancing, but it was hard enough to stun him. Eyes smarting and head swimming, Frank sank to the floor, bumping into a table as he fell.

Someone's going through my pockets! he realized. He struggled groggily to fight off whoever was bending over him. But another clout, this one on the side of the head, left him too dazed to resist.

Outside the restaurant, people stopped and gathered to stare at the emerging customers and ask what was going on. A fire siren shrieked in the distance.

"Someone must've called in an alarm," Biff said.

"Hey, where's Frank?" Joe exclaimed, running a hand through his blond hair.

The four realized that the older Hardy boy was still in the ice-cream parlor. Without hesitating, Joe plunged back into the reeking interior, followed by Tony, Biff, and Chet.

Despite the dense smoke, they were able to make out Frank's prostrate form and carry him outside, where he soon revived after a few whiffs from an oxygen inhalator supplied by the firemen.

"Want us to call an ambulance?" one asked.

"No thanks, I'm okay," Frank assured him.

As the firemen moved on to other tasks, Joe turned to his brother, his brow puckered in a slight frown. "What happened in there, Frank? Don't tell me you just passed out from the smoke?"

"No, I didn't. Someone conked me on the head."

Joe whistled and the other boys stared in amazement as Frank related the attack in the ice-cream parlor.

"Two pickpockets in one morning," Tony commented. "This town isn't safe any more!"

"The first man wasn't a pickpocket," Frank reminded him. "And maybe the second creep was after the devil doll that the first guy left."

"Are you kidding?"

"No way. It's too big a coincidence to assume the two events aren't connected."

"Maybe you'll never know," Chet said. "Now that the thing's been stolen."

"Don't worry, it's safe." Joe grinned and pulled his hand out of his pocket to reveal the sinister little figure. "I grabbed it off the table when we all got up to leave."

"Nice going!" Frank congratulated his brother. "Actually, I wasn't too sure whether the guy who slugged me had taken it, or I'd left it behind."

"What do you mean, 'nice going'?" Chet said uneasily. "If the crooks want it that much, you might get conked again!"

The fire crew was already coiling up the hoses, preparing to depart, and the smoke from the ice-cream parlor seemed to have cleared considerably. The boys now realized they had seen no flames.

"What caused all this?" Joe asked the fire captain.

"Smoke bomb. Someone tossed it through the kitchen window. There was no fire at all."

The Hardys looked at each other, both wondering the same thing. Had the smoke bomb been thrown on purpose to give the sneak thief a chance to steal the devil doll from Frank? If so, the trick had failed.

"Did you see that flat-nosed guy come back in the place?" Joe asked his brother.

Frank shook his head. "No, but he could've sent someone else in to conk me. If our hunch is right, *he* probably threw the bomb."

Joe dropped his brother off at home to rest before the boys went back to the construction site to finish their jobs. When the younger Hardy finally came back from work, he was greeted by his tall, thin Aunt Gertrude, who handed him a special delivery letter. Scrawled in ink on the envelope was THE HARDY BOYS, followed by their house number on Elm Street in Bayport, but there was no return address.

"Wonder who it's from?" Joe asked just as Frank came downstairs from their bedroom.

"What is it?" the older boy asked.

His aunt clucked impatiently. "Why not open it and find out?" Gertrude Hardy was the unmarried sister of the boys' father, the famed investigator Fenton Hardy. She lived with the family and was known as the best cook in town. Although she worried and constantly nagged Mr. Hardy and his sons about the dangers of detective work, she took a keen interest in all their cases.

Frank smiled as he realized she was as curious about the contents of the letter as he was. "Good idea, Aunty," he said and slit open the envelope.

The hall telephone rang. Joe answered it.

"You one of the Hardy boys?" said a gruff voice.

"That's right. What can I do for you?"

"Keep your grubhooks off my treasure, boy! Someday I'm coming back for that load of silver plate—and it better still be where I left it, y'understand? If it's gone, there'll be the *devil* to pay!"

"Who is this?" Joe demanded curtly.

"The Outlaw of the Pine Barrens!" came the reply, followed by a burst of maniacal laughter. Then a receiver clicked at the other end of the line.

2 A Mystery from History

Joe put down the phone with a bewildered expression.

"What was that all about?" Aunt Gertrude demanded sharply. He turned and saw that she had been eavesdropping discreetly on the brief conversation.

"Search me," he shrugged. "Something about a load of silver plate. Sounded like some nut. He called himself the Outlaw of the Pine Barrens."

"If he was telling the truth," Frank spoke up, "you've been talking to a dead man."

Joe stared at his brother. "What do you mean?"

"Take a look at this." Frank held out a sheet that he had taken from the envelope and unfolded.

Joe studied it with curiosity. It appeared to be a photostat of an old letter, crudely written in an outdated style of handwriting, with many of the words misspelled.

MARCH 3, 1781

HOPE THIS REACHES YOU TU. WILL SEND IT BY INJUN PETE CUZ HE NOES OUR HIDEOUT ON CEDAR KNOB AND SAYS HE WILL STOP THERE ON HIS WAY BACK TO PARSONS FORGE. ALSO HE CAINT READ, SO HE CAINT TELL NOBUDDY WHUT I HEV WRIT. BLACK JACK WAS TOOK BAD AND DIED. BURIED SILVER UNDER HIM FISH-HOOK TEN PACES NORTH AS CROW FLIES. COME QUIK AND WE WILL SPLIT TREASURE. GOOD LUCK, MATES.

JEM TAGGART

Joe looked up at his brother in blank amazement and passed the letter on to his aunt, who scanned it intently through her gold-rimmed glasses. "What do you make of it, Frank?" he asked.

"First tell me exactly what that weird caller said," the older Hardy boy countered.

After Joe finished, Frank puzzled over the events thoughtfully. "Both the phone call and the letter concern a silver treasure. That has to be more than a coincidence, right?"

Joe nodded. "Just like that sneak who stuck the

devil doll in your pocket, and the other sneak who tried to swipe it."

"What was that?" put in Aunt Gertrude, frowning at the boys suspiciously. "What devil doll are you talking about?"

Joe produced the tiny plastic demon to show her, and Frank briefly related the incidents Joe had referred to.

Miss Hardy shook her head as she examined the ugly little figure. "I don't like this a bit!" she fretted. "Looks absolutely nasty to me—like something right out of a horror movie!"

"I wasn't too crazy about the whole business myself," Frank replied dryly, "but I'm not sure what we can do about it, Aunty."

Turning back to Joe, Frank resumed their discussion of the letter and phone call. "You'll notice the letter also speaks of *our hideout*."

"Which sure sounds like a gang of crooks."

"Exactly! Add it all up and I'd say the chances are Jem Taggart is—or *was*—the Outlaw of the Pine Barrens."

"That figures, all right," Joe agreed. "The timing alone makes it look as though the letter and the call are connected somehow. But who's behind it all?"

"Good question. For that matter, we don't even know if this letter's authentic or a fake."

"Oh, I almost forgot!" Miss Hardy exclaimed.

"Forgot what?" asked Joe.

"You two had another call this morning while you were out, right after that special delivery letter arrived."

"Who was it?" Frank queried.

"I don't know. He didn't give me any name. In fact, he was rather gruff and impolite. His voice was sort of muffled, or—well, *distant*, as if he were rasping at the phone from far off."

"Sounds like the nut I just spoke to," said Joe. "Probably trying to sound like a ghostly voice from the grave."

"Another thing," Miss Hardy went on, encouraged by her nephews' obvious interest. "There was a car parked down the street all morning. I couldn't see who was in it, but I'm sure there was someone at the wheel. And I noticed a few moments ago when I looked out the window that it's gone. Mighty suspicious, if you ask me."

"You could be right," Frank said thoughtfully. "The driver may have parked there to watch for the special delivery. Then he could have radioed the person who made the call. Or, if he had a car phone, he could have phoned himself. When you told him we weren't home, he stuck around till he saw us come back and called again."

"That makes sense," Joe said. "The call came

right after we got here. But why? You think someone's playing a joke on us?"

"That's possible," Frank said dubiously, "but if
so, the joker has a strange sense of humor."

"And he's sure going to a lot of trouble to set us
up for laughs," Joe added wryly.

Frank nodded. "We'd better check it out."

"Okay. But where do we start?"

"Well, let's see. The Pine Barrens are in southern
New Jersey, I think—" Frank paused, frowned, and
scratched his head. "But don't ask me what went on
there in 1781."

"Hmph! You young folks still get American history in school, don't you?" Miss Hardy cut in. "Why
not ask your history teacher?"

"Say, that's a good idea!" Joe exclaimed.

"Well, don't look so surprised," she retorted. "Is
there anything all that strange about me getting a
good idea?"

Both boys burst out laughing.

"Not a thing, Aunty," Joe replied, giving her an
affectionate hug.

The boys promptly phoned their high-school
history teacher, Miss Degan, who said she would be
glad to give them whatever help she could. She
turned out to be an excellent source of information.
During the summer, she was studying to complete

her master's degree at nearby Bayshore University. Ultimately, she hoped to achieve the degree of Ph.D. and become a college professor herself, specializing in American history of the Revolutionary period.

"Now then, what's this all about?" Miss Degan inquired when the Hardy boys were seated in her study.

Frank handed her the letter and, when she had read it, asked, "Ever hear that name before?"

"Jem Taggart? Of course. He was the famous Outlaw of the Pine Barrens."

The Hardys felt a thrill of satisfaction on hearing Frank's hunch confirmed.

"What can you tell us about him—and about the Pine Barrens, Miss Degan?" put in Joe.

The teacher smiled. "That's a pretty large order, but let me try to give you a brief answer. To begin with, New Jersey has the greatest population density—that is, the most people per square mile—of any state in the Union. Yet it also has the hugest tract of undeveloped timberland east of the Mississippi—namely, the Pine Barrens."

The northern half of the Atlantic coast, she went on to explain, was so built-up and industrialized that the stretch from Boston to Richmond was almost like one continuous city. Yet sprawled right in the middle of it, almost within sight of New York's towering World Trade Center, stretched a vast expanse of wilderness called the Pine Barrens— hundreds of thousands of lonely, sandy acres of pines, oaks, and cedars.

"It's no good for farming," Miss Degan continued, "so the early settlers left it untouched. But it did have bog iron, which they forged into cannons and cannonballs during the Revolution and the War of 1812. It also bordered the ocean and had a lot of creeks and inlets, so it offered a perfect hiding place for smugglers, not to mention Tories who disagreed with the rebels, and Hessian deserters, as well as various fugitives from the law."

One of the latter, it seems, was Jem Taggart. He pretended to be both a Tory and a rebel, depending on whichever suited his nefarious plans of the moment. He preyed on both sides during the war.

"But he was finally brought to justice," Miss Degan ended. "This book will tell you about it."

She plucked a volume from her bookshelf, found the right page, and handed the open book to her two young visitors. Together, the Hardys read how Taggart and the surviving members of his dreaded gang had been captured and hanged in 1781.

"Wow! That's the same year as the date on this letter!" Joe commented.

"And it says he's supposed to have left a buried treasure, which was never found," said Frank, "consisting of a cargo of silver plate from a captured British merchant ship. Do you suppose that's the silver Jem mentions in his letter?"

"It's possible," Miss Degan said cautiously, "and I must admit the letter looks very convincing. But remember, this is only a photostat of the original, so there would be no way to test the document scientifically. I suggest you get an opinion from an expert."

"Anyone in particular you can refer us to?"

The teacher hesitated. "Well, let me see. You might try Mr. Caleb Colpitt. He's a dealer in old maps and manuscripts."

She consulted the telephone directory for his address, which she wrote down on a slip of paper and handed to the boys. Frank and Joe thanked her and left.

Frank was at the wheel of their car as they headed homeward. The boys were discussing their visit to Miss Degan, when Frank suddenly jerked his head and muttered, "I wonder what this creep's up to now?"

"What are you talking about?" Joe inquired.

"See that black station wagon? I think he's been tagging us all the way from Bayshore. Now all of a sudden he's in a big hurry!"

"Oh, oh," Joe said, alarmed. He turned back just in time to see the wagon roaring up behind them at high speed.

"Hey, Frank! I think the driver is that flat-nosed guy from the ice-cream parlor!"

"Are you sure?" Frank asked tensely, glancing in the rearview mirror for a moment. Then he trod hard on the accelerator. "I hope we can get away from him." He looked at the lonely stretch of coastal road, ideal for a possible ambush. The sudden appearance of the flat-nosed man might have been purely accidental, but both boys doubted it.

"I bet he was following us," Joe declared. "I wish I knew what he's after!"

"We might find out sooner than you think unless we can get away from him," Frank replied. "Personally, I'd rather avoid a confrontation at this spot! It's a little too isolated for me." He drove as fast as he could, trying to outdistance the black car.

But it soon became clear that their pursuer had no intention of letting the Hardys get away. The station wagon was a powerful, eight-cylinder model, and Flat Nose was recklessly floorboarding his gas pedal. Bit by bit, he drew abreast of the Hardys' sports sedan.

Suddenly there was a loud clash of metal, and their car lurched, jolting both boys to the right.

"The dirty rat's sideswiping us!" Joe blurted.

Frank nodded grimly. "Trying to force us off the road!"

From the window of the station wagon racing alongside them, they saw Flat Nose bare his teeth in a nasty grin of vindictive glee. Again he side-swiped them—*and again!*

On their right, the shoulder of the road dropped off sharply in a cliff sheering down to a gully below. Tight-lipped but calm, Frank eased his foot off the pedal and tried to slow down, but it was no use. Whether he dropped back or sought to forge ahead, Flat Nose kept them tightly penned in.

In desperation, Frank jammed his own gas pedal to the floor, hoping their sports car might have enough zip in the showdown to leave the wagon behind. But at that same moment, the black station wagon leaped ahead and cut in front of them! Frank turned the wheel and stamped on the brakes to avoid a collision. The yellow sports sedan spun out of control toward the shoulder!

3 A Face in the Crowd

There was a screech of tires and a clatter of gravel!
The Hardys froze with fear as the steep drop-off to
the gully below yawned beneath their front wheels.
Fleeting instants seemed drawn out into agonizing
minutes before their car came to a shuddering halt,
teetering on the very brink of the cliff!

The boys stared at each other, then slowly re-
leased their tension in long, gusty sighs.

"Wow!" Joe gasped. "That's what I call too close
for comfort!"

As he reached for the door handle, his brother
warned tensely, "Don't get out. You might tip us
over."

Joe turned pale. "Can you back up?"

27

"I'll try." The engine had stalled, but Frank keyed it back to life and cautiously eased the gearshift lever into reverse.

The car groaned and the wheels spun gravel, but aside from a momentary jerk there was no movement.

Joe looked uncertain. "What do we do now?"

"Call a tow truck, I guess." Frank switched on their CB radio and was soon able to contact a wrecker cruising for business. He described their location, and the tow truck driver promised to be there in ten minutes.

The black station wagon that had caused the accident had disappeared, much to the Hardys' relief. But Joe had had the presence of mind to memorize its license number, and while the boys waited for assistance, he reported it by radio to the State Police.

The wrecker soon arrived. Its driver maneuvered into position so that the rear end of his truck was only a few feet away from the Hardys' car. Then he hooked a chain to their back bumper and within a few moments pulled them to safety.

"Thanks!" both boys exclaimed, getting out.

"What were you trying to do?" their rescuer asked with a grin. "Play rocking horse?"

"Far from it," Joe retorted. "Some wise guy forced us off the road."

The Hardys' car radio buzzed. Joe went to answer it while Frank paid the tow truck driver. The call was from the State Police, reporting that the license number that Frank had taken down belonged to a station wagon that had been stolen only an hour or so earlier, and had just been found abandoned on a highway near Bayport.

"Thanks, Sergeant, that was fast work!" Joe replied. He passed the news on to his brother, adding in disgust, "So much for our chances of identifying Flat Nose!"

"Don't worry, something tells me we haven't seen the last of him," Frank said dryly as they started home again. "But one thing we know for sure—those guys play rough!"

When they arrived home, the boys learned from their slim, attractive mother that they had had a telephone call from a newspaper reporter named Grimes.

"What did he want, Mom?" Frank asked.

"To interview you and Joe. I didn't encourage him, because I know how you and your father feel about publicity. But he was very persistent and said he'd drop around anyhow."

The Hardys had not long to wait. Less than half an hour later, the doorbell rang. Their visitor, a curly-haired man in his thirties, dressed in a rather rumpled suit, introduced himself as Nate Grimes.

Frank let him in, more out of politeness than from any desire to be interviewed.

"You write for the *Bayport Press*?" he asked the reporter.

"No. Atlantic News Service. I'm what they call a stringer, more or less a freelance correspondent."

"What can we do for you?" Joe said, trying to keep the interview as brief and as businesslike as possible.

"Is it true that you have a clue to a famous treasure? I mean the silver that was buried by the Outlaw of the Pine Barrens a couple of hundred years ago."

There was a moment of startled silence. Frank's eyes narrowed as he asked, "Where did you hear that?"

"An anonymous phone tip. I figured it might be good for a feature story, so I called to ask for this interview." Grimes studied the boys' faces intently before pressing, "Well, is it true?"

"In a way, yes," Frank admitted. "We've received a copy of an old letter that may have been written by Jem Taggart to other members of his gang, and it does mention some buried silver."

Grimes was watching Frank's expression eagerly. "Do you think the letter's on the up and up?"

Frank shrugged. "Hard to say. It looks authentic, but we're no experts."

"What about your father?" Grimes pressed. "Can't he tell if it's phony or not?"

"Perhaps. But he's busy with his own case load."

"Hey, that's right," Grimes said. "You two seem so young to be detectives, I keep forgetting you've grown up in the business, so to speak. Must be exciting, being in on all of those sensational cases he investigates. What's he working on now, by the way?"

"Sorry, we're not allowed to discuss that."

Fenton Hardy had once been an ace manhunter for the New York Police Department. Later he retired to the pleasant seaside town of Bayport to become a private investigator. Many of his cases had made national and even international head-lines, but Frank and Joe had long since learned to emulate their father's tight-lipped "no comment" attitude on such matters. By his own example, the famed sleuth had taught them the importance not only of preventing security leaks, but also of safe-guarding clients' privacy.

If Nate Grimes was put out by the boys' evident distaste for publicity, he gave no sign of it. Instead, he kept pelting them with questions about the Pine Barrens mystery.

"What's your own opinion, Mr. Grimes?" Joe said, deftly turning the focus of the quiz on their interrogator. "Do you think there's really a valuable treasure hidden out there in the woods?"

The newsman chuckled and ran his fingers through his curly hair. "You've got me there, pal— and, incidentally, make it Nate, please, not Mr. Grimes. To tell you the truth, I'd never even heard of this Outlaw character until I got that anonymous phone call. Guess I'll have to read up on him before I write my story."

"Might be a good idea," Joe commented dryly.

"Do you think that letter of Taggart's will start you off on a treasure hunt?" Grimes went on.

"I doubt it," Frank said. "But anything's possible."

In case they actually did decide to search for the outlaw's silver trove, they did not want to volunteer any information that could stir up a swarm of other treasure hunters.

After probing a bit more, Grimes asked permission to snap a few pictures of the boys and finally left.

"Nosy guy, wasn't he?" Joe remarked as they watched their visitor drive off.

Frank grinned wryly. "Guess that's what makes a good reporter."

"Hmph! If you two have nothing better to do than stare out of the window, I have a good suggestion," a tart voice broke in. "The front lawn's about a week overdue for mowing, and the bushes could do with some trimming, too!"

"Okay, we get the picture, Aunt Gertrude," Joe said, adding a surprise kiss and squeeze that left Miss Hardy tut-tutting sharply, but unable to repress a pleased smile at her nephew's obvious affection.

"If you think that'll get you an extra big slice of devil's food cake tonight, young man, you're absolutely right!" she muttered.

Twenty minutes later, as the power mower was humming across the grass and the hedge trimmer clipping away busily at the shrubbery, a white station wagon pulled up at the curb.

"Hey, it's Iola and Callie!" Joe exclaimed, stopping the mower.

The blond girl at the wheel smiled and waved, while her pert, dark-haired companion brandished several pink tickets as the Hardy boys hurried over to greet their girlfriends.

"What've you got there, Iola?" Joe asked.

"Tickets to the Turnerville Three concert tonight, over in Shoreham," the pixie-faced brunette informed him. "Want to come? You're both invited."

"You bet!" Frank said. "How'd you get the tickets? We heard they were sold out."

The Turnerville Three was a popular recording group. Iola, who was Chet Morton's sister, explained proudly that she had sold the group one of her driftwood sculptures. The musicians had been so enthusiastic over her work that they had tipped her with three pairs of tickets to their local concert. Iola had been spending the summer polishing and mounting her driftwood creations, which she sold from a stand in front of the Morton farm.

She blushed a little in spite of herself as Frank's date, Callie Shaw, spoke up. "You two didn't know we had such an artistic genius in our midst, did you?"

"Oh, yes, I did," Joe said, patting Iola gently on the shoulder. "That's really great. Is Chet coming?"

"No, he can't be bothered," Iola replied. "He's too busy with his latest hobby, so we asked Biff and Karen."

"Great! What time should we call for you?"

"You won't have to. Callie's mom said we could have the station wagon. That way we can all go in one car."

"I'll honk at seven," put in Callie. "Be ready."

"Have I ever kept you waiting?" Frank chuckled. "Don't worry!"

That evening, after the young people left the Hardy home, traffic seemed unusually heavy as the white station wagon moved along in the line of cars on the highway to Shoreham.

"I must be watching too many mystery shows on TV," Callie murmured.

"How come?" Frank asked.

"I have this strange feeling that we're being followed," she replied with a nervous giggle.

"Probably some secret admirer who wants to ask you for a date," Joe suggested jokingly.

"Not while I'm around," said Frank. "What kind of a car is this romantic creep driving, Callie?"

"Oh, I don't know! I'm not even sure what color it is. I just keep seeing the same windshield and grille in my rearview mirror every so often!"

The Hardy boys exchanged quick glances, both thinking uneasily that Callie's suspicions might not be due only to her imagination. However, neither wanted to say anything that might alarm their companions and perhaps spoil their evening. Instead, they began watching the traffic, alert for any possible tail car. But none appeared.

It was not yet seven-thirty when the three young couples reached the downtown section of Shoreham. Callie parked the station wagon in a nearby lot, and they walked to the Strand Theater where the concert was to take place.

A sign announced that the doors would open at ten minutes to eight, but a noisy crowd had already gathered outside and seemed to be growing larger every moment. Fans not lucky enough to have purchased tickets were bidding for them at inflated prices. Hawkers elbowed their way about, offering T-shirts bearing likenesses of the Turnerville Three, as well as posters, fan magazines, and other souvenirs.

"What a madhouse!" exclaimed Iola. She had to raise her voice to make herself heard.

"Let's hope it's quieter inside," Joe responded, "or we won't even be able to hear the concert!"

"Don't worry," said Biff. "Once they turn on the amplifiers, the sound'll be booming off the walls!"

Frank was about to add a good-natured wisecrack about the advisability of wearing earplugs, when he caught a glimpse of a face that froze him to instant attention. The crowd was mostly composed of young people, but the face he had just seen was that of an older man with beetling brows and a drooping black mustache.

"Hey, Joe!" he hissed, clutching his brother's arm.

"What's up, Frank?"

"See that guy with the black mustache?"

"What about him?"

"I think he's the one who stuck the devil doll in my pocket!"

The man was trying to worm his way through the crowd toward the Hardys. Frank eyed him intently,

feeling there was something strangely familiar about him.

But suddenly the man's face registered alarm. He turned abruptly and ran back the way he had come!

"I'm going after him!" Frank exclaimed and began pushing in pursuit.

4 A Sinister Suspect

Frank looked back over his shoulder as he ran, wondering what had caused the man to turn around and flee. He caught a glimpse of a red-haired fellow who was holding a folded-up newspaper and pointing it toward the mustached man in front of him.

As the fugitive broke away from the crowd, Frank heard something whiz past his ear, followed by a sharp thump just ahead. He stopped short with a gasp as he saw a deadly looking steel dart burying itself in one of the big framed posters on the gate leading to the theater parking lot.

The boy felt a chill run down his spine at the sight of the lethal missile. Had it been aimed at him or the stranger with the black mustache? Either way, he was convinced he had narrowly escaped a serious injury, or death!

By now the crowd was milling about more excitedly than ever, even though most of the people had no idea of what had happened.

Frank made a desperate effort to go after the man with the black mustache, but the fellow was already lost to view.

Finally, the young detective got clear of the crowd and darted down the street, glancing in every direction. It was no use. The mustached man had disappeared.

Disgusted, Frank went to rejoin the others. As he approached his companions, the theater doors opened and the eager fans began pouring inside. Frank met up with Joe, Biff, and their dates to the right of the entrance.

"Good grief! What was that all about?" Callie asked him anxiously.

"Tell you later," said Frank, squeezing her hand, not wanting to worry her. "Come on, we'd better go inside before the concert starts, or some of these eager beavers may grab our reserved seats!"

The dart, he turned around to check, was gone. He guessed that the red-haired assailant had plucked it out of the poster as Frank pursued the man with the dark mustache.

The cheering inside the auditorium made it

nearly impossible to carry on a conversation, and once the concert started, the amplifiers boomed as loudly as Biff had predicted. The Hardys and their friends had to shout in each other's ears to be heard. Frank and Joe were just as glad to postpone their explanation to the girls, knowing the story might stop them from enjoying the performance.

Not until the concert was over and they were parked in a hamburger drive-in on the road to Bayport, did the young detectives tell Callie, Iola, and Karen the whole story.

"Oh, my goodness!" Iola gulped. "I had no idea it was that serious!"

Callie, too, had turned pale. "Do you believe the dart was meant for you, Frank?"

The older Hardy boy shook his head. "No. The more I think about it, the more I'm convinced it was fired at that man with the black mustache. He knew the red-headed guy had spotted him. That's why he turned and ran away. The funny thing is, I have a feeling I've seen that mustached man before somewhere."

"You mean, before he stuck that devil doll in your pocket?" Karen inquired.

Frank nodded, frowning thoughtfully. "Don't ask me why, but his face just looked familiar, somehow. For that matter, I have a hunch we've seen the other guy before, too."

"The redhead?" Joe shot a glance at his brother.

"Yes. In fact, I seem to connect them up in my mind, as if I saw them about the same time—"

His voice was trailing off when suddenly his eyes widened and he snapped his fingers. "Now I remember! I saw him at the ice-cream place. He was one of the customers who came in after that flat-nosed guy left!"

"Wow! Then the two of them could have been in cahoots on the smoke-bomb caper!" Joe said.

"Sure. He probably was sent in to shout 'Fire!' in order to set off a panic when smoke started billowing out of the kitchen."

"But why are they still trailing us?"

"Maybe they're hoping to get back the devil doll," Frank theorized. "Or wait, come to think of it, maybe they even figured that sooner or later we'd lead them to the man with the black mustache!"

Both Joe and Biff looked startled.

"In that case," Biff said, "they sure figured right!"

When Frank and Joe arrived home that night, they were surprised to find their mother and Aunt Gertrude waiting up for them. Mrs. Hardy looked uneasy, and even her sharp-tongued, stiff-necked sister-in-law seemed a trifle disturbed.

"Anything wrong, Mom?" Joe asked.

"I hope not, dear, but Gertrude and I had a

notion that someone was spying on the house tonight."

"It was more than a notion, Laura," Miss Hardy corrected. "We both saw that fellow skulking in the shadows!"

"Whereabouts, Aunty?" asked Frank.

"First we sighted him across the street, standing by that big, old elm tree on the corner. Later on we glimpsed him going through the alley, peering over the back fence."

"What did he look like?"

"It was too dark to tell, but I'm sure it was the same man."

Both ladies admitted they were worried. But they had decided against calling the police, since the prowler could no longer be seen and had evidently given up his vigil for the night.

"We'd better make sure," Frank said, and Joe agreed.

The two boys armed themselves with powerful flashlights and searched around the vicinity of the house, but found no one. Switching on the burglar alarm system, they then turned off all the downstairs lights and settled down for a vigil of their own, keeping a lookout through various windows. No prowler appeared, however, so the boys finally went to bed.

After breakfast the next morning, Frank and Joe drove to the shop of Caleb Colpitt, the dealer in old maps and manuscripts whom their history teacher had mentioned.

His place of business was located in a weather-beaten frame building in one of the older sections of Bayport. Several ornate maps, one of them dating back to the early 1700s, were displayed in glass cases in the window. The Hardy boys guessed that these were removed frequently or shifted to different positions, so as not to expose them to too much sunlight.

Colpitt himself was a tall, spare, balding man who wore sleeve garters and was dressed in a rather old-fashioned way. When Frank and Joe introduced themselves, he recognized their names at once and said that he had helped their father some years ago on a case involving a stolen rare map.

"That's great, Mr. Colpitt," said Frank. "Then maybe you won't mind helping us, too."

"Be glad to, if I can."

"First," Frank handed him the photostat of Jem Taggart's letter, "would you say the letter this was copied from was authentic?"

"H'm." Caleb Colpitt proceeded to study the sheet carefully for two or three minutes, using a large, square magnifying glass to aid in his examination. "It certainly *appears* to be genuine," he announced cautiously at length, "or if not, then it was forged with a great deal of expertise. For example, the way certain letters of the alphabet are formed here would require the forger to know a good deal about the handwriting of the period, or at any rate more than the average person knows. I'm afraid there's no way to tell for sure, however, without seeing the original parchment and subjecting it to various tests."

Looking up with a slight frown, he added, "Of course, even without the original, you could probably get a much more reliable opinion from a trained examiner of questionable documents."

"Your opinion's good enough for us, Mr. Colpitt. At least it'll serve for the time being," Frank replied. "Next, would you have an old map in stock showing the Pine Barrens area of New Jersey during Colonial times?"

The elderly map dealer looked startled. "How odd that you should ask me that!"

"How come, sir?" Joe asked.

"It so happens I did have a detailed map of that very area that was drawn for the Continental Army in 1778."

"That sounds just like what we need! Where is it now, Mr. Colpitt?"

"I wish I knew! Someone broke into my shop the night before last and stole it!"

5 *The Angry Visitor*

The same suspicion struck both of the Hardy boys.
The map might have been stolen by someone who
was hoping to find Jem Taggart's buried treasure!

Caleb Colpitt saw the look that passed between
them. "You're wondering if the theft may have
anything to do with that letter you just showed me,
aren't you?" he inquired shrewdly.

"How did you guess?" Joe blurted.

"The whole story's in the morning paper."

The boys realized the map dealer was referring to
Nate Grimes's report of their interview.

"As you can see," Frank pointed out to Mr.
Colpitt, "this letter says the gang's hideout was on
Cedar Knob. Well, we've looked in Dad's big atlas

at home and also on an automobile map of New Jersey, but neither one shows any place by that name."

"For that matter," Joe added, "neither one shows Parson's Forge, either. We did find the name in a book about the Pine Barrens that our history teacher showed us, but even the map in that book didn't have Cedar Knob on it."

Mr. Colpitt nodded. "A good many old names die out, especially in an area as lonely and off the beaten track as the Pine Barrens."

"How would the thief have known you had such a map?" Frank asked.

Colpitt explained that it had recently been on display in his shop window.

"Was anything else taken?"

The map dealer shook his head. "Just that one item."

"That sure does sound as if the thief knew exactly what he was after," Joe agreed. "And the robbery occurred the night before last?"

"That's right. I discovered what had happened when I came in yesterday morning."

"Then if there *is* any connection, the burglar must have known about Taggart's letter before Joe and I got this copy by special delivery yesterday."

"Wouldn't be too surprising," the elderly map dealer remarked dryly. "After all, if the letter's authentic, it was written two centuries ago, so a good many people may have seen it by now."

"True," Frank said, "but I have a hunch it may have come to light just recently."

"Getting back to the geographic question," Joe put in, "do you have any other maps that might show the New Jersey Pine Barrens?"

"H'm. Well now, I do have one that might be worth checking." Colpitt disappeared into the back room and soon returned, bringing a map enclosed in transparent plastic. It had evidently been drawn during the Civil War period to show the area of military operations in Virginia and Pennsylvania, but also included the southern portion of New Jersey.

Colpitt and the boys scanned it eagerly. Joe was the first to spot the landmark. "There it is!" He stabbed his finger at the name CEDAR KNOB inscribed on the map in tiny letters.

The Hardys were jubilant, feeling they had now taken the first successful step toward finding the lost treasure.

"Mind if we copy this, Mr. Colpitt?" Frank asked.

"Not at all. Here's a piece of paper."

Joe whipped out a pen and sketched enough of the surrounding terrain and place names to enable them to find the spot without difficulty.

Frank, meanwhile, had another spur-of-the-moment inspiration. Pulling the devil doll out of his pocket, he showed it to the old map dealer.

"Ever see anything like that before, sir?"

Colpitt picked up his magnifying glass again to study the ugly little plastic figure.

"No, can't say I have," he said at last. "But it looks like some sort of heraldic beast."

"You mean like you see on coats of arms?"

"That's right, like unicorns and dragons and griffins, that sort of thing. There's a woman named Mrs. Amanda Hertford who traces people's genealogy and family coats of arms. She might be able to help you. Don't know her address, but you can find her in the phone book."

The Hardys thanked the elderly map dealer and left the shop. Before driving off, they called their three buddies, Chet Morton, Tony Prito, and Biff Hooper, and arranged to meet them for lunch at the Bayport Diner.

Chet was already ensconced in a booth, munching on a cheeseburger, when Frank and Joe arrived.

"Hope you don't mind my ordering before you got here," the plump youth said between mouthfuls. "I was really famished!"

"So what else is new?" Frank said, grinning at his brother.

"This story, for one thing," Chet retorted. Taking a rolled-up newspaper from the seat beside him, he flipped it out flat on the table so the Hardys could see their picture and Grimes's account of their interview on the front page. "Boy, you guys really have a knack for making news."

"We didn't ask the reporter to come around," Joe informed their friend as Biff and Tony walked in. "Somebody tipped him off."

The boys listened avidly as Frank filled them in on everything that had happened.

"Another mystery case!" Chet exclaimed, wiping his mouth with a napkin and signaling the waitress. "I knew it right off when Iola told me about that dart business last night!"

"You think there's any connection between this treasure letter and the devil doll?" Tony asked after the waitress had taken everyone's order.

Frank shrugged. "We don't have any evidence so far, except for the timing."

"And don't forget Flat Nose tailing us after we left Miss Degan's place," Joe put in.

But Frank shook his head doubtfully. "That doesn't prove anything. He could have shadowed us all the way from Bayport. Whatever's behind it all, though, it's pretty strange, getting mixed up with *two* sets of weirdos at the same time!"

"Well, anyhow, we do have one clue," said Joe.

"What's that?" Biff asked.

"We've located the place where the Outlaw of the

Pine Barrens and his gang hid out. So would you like to go treasure hunting with us?"

"Sure! How soon do we start?" Biff asked, and Tony exclaimed, "Count me in!"

"Me, too!" Chet said enthusiastically.

"Joe and I would like to get going tomorrow," Frank told them, and the five Bayporters hastily laid plans for the expedition. When they finally returned to Elm Street, the Hardys saw a flashy-looking, high-powered car parked in front of their house. A tall, balding man, presumably its driver, was standing on the porch, engaged in an argument with Aunt Gertrude.

As the boys approached, the man turned and glared at them. "Oh, so there they are!" he growled belligerently.

Ignoring him, Frank asked his aunt what was going on.

"A loud, unpleasant nuisance, that's what!" Miss Hardy snapped. "This rude individual came blasting away at the doorbell as if I was deaf, and then he demanded to see you boys. When I told him you weren't here, he tried to bully his way inside and threatened to make a scene unless I told him where he could get hold of you!"

Frank stared at the man coldly. "Well, here we are. What is it you want?"

"That letter of Jem Taggart's you two smart alecks

filched from my client!" The stranger was red-faced with anger as he hissed out the words.

"Watch what you're saying," the elder Hardy boy retorted. "I don't let anyone get away with calling us thieves. Before this goes any further, maybe you'd better tell us who you are."

"Verrill. Ambrose Verrill, attorney-at-law!"

"If you really are an attorney, then you ought to know better than to go around making wild accusations. It could either get you a lawsuit for slander or a punch in the mouth. Now if you can calm down and tell us what this is all about, come on inside and we'll listen."

Frank himself was angry enough to come to blows with their unpleasant visitor, and he could sense that Joe's quick temper was even nearer to the boiling point. On the other hand, he was eager to hear what the man had to say in the hope that his story might yield a clue to the mysterious sender of the Outlaw's letter.

Verrill swallowed hard, trying to get himself under control. "Very well," he huffed. "I'll give you a chance to clear this up, but you'd better come clean and talk fast!"

Joe could barely wait till they were seated in the front room to reply in a sizzling voice, "For your information, we have nothing to come clean about! You're the one who'd better talk fast!"

"According to the morning paper," Verrill began, "you have a letter, dated March 3, 1781, from the Outlaw of the Pine Barrens to other members of his gang. Correct or incorrect?"

"The story's accurate," Frank said curtly. "What about it?"

"You have no right to that letter! It's none of your affair!"

"Apparently you didn't read the news report very carefully. We don't have the original letter. What came to us through the mail was a photostat."

"Copy or not, makes no difference. What counts is the information contained in the letter. I don't want that circulating to every Tom, Dick, and Harry. So hand it over!"

At this outburst, the Hardys merely looked at each other and maintained a scornful silence.

Verrill rose to his feet, his face more flushed than ever. "For the last time, I want that letter. It belongs to my client, and it's my responsibility!"

"So you keep telling us," Frank replied. "I don't know if you take us for simpletons, but we'll need more than your word for that. The way you've been acting, it's hard to believe you're even a lawyer. Have you any idea who sent that copy of Taggart's letter to us, or why?"

"I don't have to answer any questions, young man! You're the ones in possession of stolen property. You'd better clear that up first, if you know what's good for you!" Ambrose Verrill shook his finger at the boys to emphasize his point. "Have you got some half-baked notion of hunting for that treasure?" Verrill paused, and when the boys did not answer, repeated more loudly, "Well, have you?"

"We don't have to answer any questions, either!" Joe blurted, stung by the man's hectoring tone.

"Let me tell you right now," Verrill ranted, "if you poke your noses into the Pine Barrens, interfering with my client's search, you'll be sorry!"

Frank sprang up from his chair, his eyes blazing. "Don't threaten us, Mr. Verrill! We've heard just about enough from you."

"Just remember what I said!" Verrill blustered and went out the front door and down the porch steps. A moment or two later they heard his car speed off.

"Well, I never!" Gertrude Hardy sniffed. She had been listening discreetly to the conversation from the archway leading into the dining room. "If that man's a lawyer, he should be disbarred!"

"I'd like to disbar his nose!" Joe gritted, clenching his fists.

"Are you two really going to look for the Outlaw's treasure?" their aunt added, curious.

"We'll give it a try!" Frank told her with a grin, "but don't worry about Verrill."

"Hmph!" Miss Hardy sniffed. "Loudmouthed bullies like him don't worry me. But there may be more to this treasure business than meets the eye!"

"We'll be careful," Joe promised. "And now we'd better make a list of all the items we need for our expedition."

Frank nodded. "We'll have to get our camping gear together. Our sleeping bags are still at Biff's house. I'll call him and tell him to pack them."

"Didn't you say there was a rip in your tent?" Aunt Gertrude inquired.

Frank snapped his fingers. "That's right. I forgot all about it."

"I'll fix it for you," his aunt offered.

Frank gave her an affectionate hug. "Aunt Gertrude, you're the greatest. What would we ever do without you?"

"I wonder." Aunt Gertrude chuckled.

When the young detectives had all their equipment ready, Frank telephoned Mrs. Amanda Hertford, the lady whom Caleb Colpitt had mentioned, and asked if they could see her. After shopping for supplies, the Hardys drove to her house.

She turned out to be a gray-haired woman with an open, pleasant manner. When Frank showed her the devil doll, she studied it carefully, then shook her head and frowned. "No, I don't believe this represents any heraldic beast. Still, it does seem familiar somehow. Wait a minute."

Mrs. Hertford took down several large books of heraldry and began leafing through them, looking for a picture of any similar creature, but without success.

Suddenly she stopped short and snatched up the little plastic figure. Her eyes lit up as she looked at it again. "Of course! Now I remember where I saw this before!"

6 Art for Sale

"Where, Mrs. Hertford?" Frank asked eagerly.

"It was a roadside stand, not very far from here. Let me see now, where was it?"

"You mean, someone was *selling* a devil doll like this?" Joe broke in.

"No, it wasn't this small. It was a ceramic statuette, maybe about a foot high."

"But the same sort of creature?" Frank pursued.

"Yes, definitely, with bat wings, just like this one has, and a devil's tail and the same kind of snout and claws. If only I could place it!"

The Hardys glanced at each other in surprise, while Mrs. Hertford knit her brows, trying to recall the exact location of the roadside stand.

"Old Orchard Road, that's it!" she exclaimed suddenly. "Somewhere on the right side. I saw it as I was driving into Bayport this morning. I'm afraid I can't be much more specific than that."

"That's specific enough, Mrs. Hertford. You've been a big help!" Frank exclaimed gratefully.

The boys thanked her and hurried back to their car. Just as they were about to start out for Old Orchard Road, the dashboard radio buzzed and a red light blinked, indicating a transmission on their special frequency.

The caller proved to be Aunt Gertrude.

"What's up, Aunty?" Joe queried.

"You boys have a client. Male, well-dressed, about forty. Sounds as though his case might be important."

"We'll be there in ten minutes. Over and out."

Postponing their business on Old Orchard Road temporarily, the Hardys drove straight home to Elm Street. Their client proved to be a quiet-mannered, pipe-smoking man in a tweed jacket who gave his name as Ogden Price.

"How can we help you?" Frank inquired as he and Joe sat down on the sofa, facing their visitor.

"By finding my cousin, Rupert Price."

"Is he missing," Joe asked, "or have you just lost touch with him?"

"He disappeared twenty years ago."

58

"How come you waited so long to trace him?"

"Because an uncle of ours died recently, leaving him a valuable inheritance, which he'll lose if he's not found. Also, I read in the morning papers that you may be going to the Pine Barrens, and I've a hunch that's where Rupert's hiding."

Frank frowned. "Hiding from what?"

"The law—or so he thinks. Actually, he's been in the clear for years."

"Maybe you'd better tell us the whole story."

Ogden Price nodded, rubbing the bowl of his pipe against his cheek and staring unhappily at the carpet. "It started when my cousin was accused of killing a man. They'd had a bitter quarrel over a business deal and the police proved that Rupe had been in the man's office just a short time before he was found dead. The evidence seemed pretty over-whelming. In fact, there was a warrant out for Rupe's arrest. When he came to me for help, I turned him down."

There was a moment's silence before Joe said, "You didn't believe he was innocent?"

"No. I was convinced he was guilty. On top of which, we'd never gotten along with each other, so I didn't want any part of the whole mess. I advised him to give himself up. Instead, when the police came to arrest him for the murder, he gave them the slip and disappeared."

"But since then, you say he's been cleared?" Frank questioned.

"Yes. Later on the real killer confessed. He was convicted and my Cousin Rupert's name was cleared. Trouble is, the case was a couple of years old when it was finally solved, so at that time it didn't get nearly as much attention in the press as it did when the murder was headline news. Rupe probably has no idea the police have stopped looking for him."

"What makes you think he went to the Pine Barrens?"

Ogden Price shrugged. "It's just a hunch. But Rupe went canoeing there several times, and I remember him remarking what a vast, lonely, unspoiled region it was, and how a man could hole up there as long as he liked. Rupe loved the wilderness and the outdoors, you see. That's why it seems natural that he'd go there to hide out."

Joe said, "How about the inheritance you mentioned?"

Price paused to relight his pipe before replying. "Well, it consists of both money and property. I can't give you an exact figure, but my uncle's lawyer estimates the estate will amount to over a million dollars."

Joe whistled. "Wow! That's a lot of money!"

"Indeed, it is," Price agreed.

"How much of that will go to your cousin?"

"I'm to get two hundred and fifty thousand. The rest will go to Rupert, to help make up for the injustice and unhappiness he's suffered. But if he doesn't show up to claim his bequest, then I'll inherit everything, since neither Rupe nor my uncle have any other living relatives."

"So if we find him," Frank pointed out, "it'll cost you three-quarter of a million dollars."

"That's one way of looking at it, I suppose."

"A lot of people wouldn't want to give away that big a fortune," Joe said. "If you don't mind my asking, how come you feel differently?"

Again their visitor shrugged. "If you want the truth, I'm ashamed of myself for not helping Rupe when he was first accused of the murder. At least I should have been willing to give him the benefit of the doubt. Since I didn't—well, the least I can do for him now is to find him and see that he gets his share of my uncle's estate." Ogden Price puffed on his pipe, then added with a dry smile, "As for the money itself, two hundred and fifty thousand is quite enough for me, thank you. I never married, and so I don't have a family to worry about."

The Hardys were silent for a few moments, mulling over the details of the case.

"How'll we know your cousin if we do find him?" Frank asked at length. "He may have changed a good deal in twenty years, let alone the fact that he's probably going under an assumed name."

"That's true," Ogden Price conceded. "All I can do is show you the last photograph I have of him."

He took a snapshot out of his pocket and handed it to the boys. It showed a lean, dark-haired young man in the uniform of a United States Navy medical corpsman.

"Rupe enlisted while he was in college," Price explained. "He was hoping to save up enough money to put himself through medical school. But instead, he found himself facing a murder rap only a few months after he got out of the service. It was a tough break, all right—I just hope it hasn't broken his spirit."

"Can you think of any other clues or leads that may help us identify him?" said Joe.

"Well, let me see." Ogden Price frowned thoughtfully as he shook the cinders out of his pipe into an ashtray. "His favorite pastime was whittling and woodcarving. That's not much to go on, but it's about the only thing that comes to mind."

"Okay, Mr. Price, we'll see what we can do," Frank promised. "Where can we reach you if we do turn up any information?"

Price wrote out his address, then shook hands with the Hardys and left. A few minutes later, after telling their mother and Aunt Gertrude about the new case they had just taken on, the boys hurried out to their yellow sports sedan and headed for Old Orchard Road.

They had driven only a short distance when Frank suddenly gasped and stepped on the brakes. "Joe! Do you see what I see?"

"I'll say I do! The greatest sculptor since Michelangelo—and I do mean greatest! In size, that is."

As Joe spoke, Frank was already swinging left into the driveway of the Morton farm.

On a stand nearby were several examples of Iola's driftwood sculpture, and a red ceramic statuette in the likeness of the devil doll! At a separate wooden table, Chet was molding a bust out of wet clay. He was wearing an artist's smock and a French beret.

A large sign tacked to the display stand said:

HAVE YOURSELF IMORTALIZED BY
A FAMOUS SCULPTER—$2.00!
ARTIST WILL POSE FOR SNAPSHOTS
WHILE HE WORKS—25¢

Chet greeted the Hardys as they jumped out of their car. "Want me to make busts of you guys?"

"Are you kidding?" Frank exclaimed. "One joke is enough around here!"

Chet's moonface fell. "Of course, if you don't appreciate art, that's your business," he said huffily.

"Just don't make fun of what you don't understand!"

The tubby youth perked up, however, as Frank picked up his red devil doll to admire it. "Not bad, except that you brought us here on a wild-goose chase."

"How come?"

"A lady told us about this, and we thought we had a hot lead on the real devil doll. When'd you make it, Chet?"

"Yesterday afternoon. Then I had it baked and glazed over at the Fair Hills Kiln. Pretty good likeness, just working from memory, huh?"

"Very good, I have to admit. You may be a sculptor yet, pal—if you can just learn to spell the word. And, incidentally, there should be two *m*'s in *immortalized*."

Chet flushed slightly with embarrassment, "Listen, you can't expect an artist to be talented at *everything*!"

With his eyes twinkling, Joe asked, "Any takers yet on your offer to pose for snapshots?"

"Not yet—but plenty of people slowed down to stare at me! And one wise guy snapped me without even paying!"

The Hardys burst out laughing and Chet looked surprised. Then he grinned good-naturedly. "Why don't you come in for a snack?" he offered, and the young detectives accepted gladly. After refreshing themselves with some pie à la mode, the Hardys started home.

That night, shortly after everyone had retired, the burglar alarm went off at the Hardy house. Frank and Joe were out of bed in an instant.

Both grabbed heavy, powerful flashlights. Not only would their beams blind an intruder, but in an emergency, the devices could be wielded as defensive weapons.

Outside their father's study, the boys paused for a moment while Frank gently took hold of the doorknob. Then he turned it suddenly and flung the door wide open, while they flashed their beams into the room.

A tall figure who had just finished climbing through the window, froze in the brilliant glare!

Frank gasped as he recognized the intruder. He was the person who had thrust the devil doll into his pocket and later had appeared outside the theater where the concert was being held—*the man with the drooping black mustache!*

7 El Diablo

There was a moment of tense silence as the boys stared at the intruder. Then the man slowly reached up to his mustache and pulled it off!

Seconds later, his bushy black eyebrows had also been peeled away!

"Dad!" Joe exclaimed.

"Right, Son!" Fenton Hardy, tall and strongly built, chuckled and held out his arms as the two boys rushed to share his hearty embrace.

"It's great to see you, Dad!" Frank said.

Hearing the happy outburst of voices, the women ventured downstairs and were soon caught up in the excitement of Mr. Hardy's return, while Joe quickly went to turn off the alarm.

"Why'd you slip that little devil doll in my

pocket, Dad?" Frank asked when he was able to make himself heard.

"Well, it's a long story, Son—"

"And you're not going to tell it till you've had a chance to sit down and catch your breath!" Miss Hardy interrupted in her usual sharp, scolding voice. "So I suggest you all adjourn to the kitchen while I make some cocoa!"

"Sounds like a mighty good idea, Gertrude!" The detective grinned, winking at the two boys, and slipping an arm around his wife's shoulders.

Later, as they sat around the table, Mr. Hardy began, "As you've gathered by now, I've been operating strictly undercover lately. It's all part of a coast-to-coast manhunt for a deadly international crook known as El Diablo."

"That's Spanish for 'The Devil,' isn't it?" Mrs. Hardy asked.

"Right, Laura. According to most accounts, he's Latin American, which explains the Spanish nickname—and believe me, he's really earned it!"

"What's he accused of?" Joe broke in.

"Among other crimes, large-scale smuggling, the infiltration of foreign spies into the U.S.A., disposing of stolen goods overseas, illegal exporting of technical electronic gear, and—well, I could go on with quite a list, but that'll give you the general idea, I believe," Mr. Hardy replied.

A nationwide dragnet by the FBI, Mr. Hardy related, had so far proved fruitless, so they had called him in to aid their search.

"Any leads to go on?" asked Frank.

"So far, just one that amounts to anything, at least in my opinion. Recently, a crook named Kerric, who's been on the FBI's 'Most Wanted' list, was picked up in the New Jersey Pine Barrens under odd circumstances."

At mention of the Pine Barrens, Frank and Joe exchanged startled glances, but neither wanted to interrupt their father's story.

"A state trooper happened to pull into a gas station down there," Mr. Hardy went on, "when he saw this fellow walking along the road. The trooper spotted him as Kerric and arrested him. Now, I'd already picked up some underworld rumors indicating that Kerric was mixed up with El Diablo. When they questioned him, Kerric absolutely refused to talk—they couldn't break him down, but they did find that little devil doll in his pocket."

Frank hurried out of the kitchen to get the sinister plastic figure and laid it on the table for everyone to see.

"How scary looking!" Mrs. Hardy murmured.

"This El Diablo character may be the head of a band of devil worshipers!" her sister-in-law declared. "Have you considered that possibility, Fenton?"

"Not very seriously, Gertrude. But I can tell you this. I've flashed that ugly little doll a number of times in various dives and hangouts where members of the underworld tend to congregate. Whenever I do, it seems to startle everyone who sees it, and more than once I've heard the name *El Diablo* being whispered behind my back."

"Have you tried to get any crooks to talk about it?" Frank asked. "Just casually, I mean."

"I have, in all sorts of ways," Mr. Hardy replied, "but invariably they clam up. It's obvious they're scared out of their wits for fear Diablo or one of his gang may spot them as squealers."

Mr. Hardy explained that after letting himself be seen carrying the devil doll and mentioning the name, El Diablo, in a big-city café frequented by mobsters and other known crooks, he found himself being stalked by two hoodlums—one red-haired, the other easily spotted by his flat nose.

"They even trailed me here to Bayport," the private investigator told his anxious listeners. "I figured they were about to jump me. But if it came to a fight or a gun in my back, I didn't want to risk them getting away with the devil doll—especially since that was the only clue I had. When I happened to see you boys with your friends, I decided the safest bet was to try and slip it into one of your pockets."

"The only trouble was, those two hoods saw you do it," put in Frank, "probably because I reacted so sharply. I thought you were a pickpocket!"

Mr. Hardy frowned with concern as his two sons gave him a full account of their recent adventures. He was particularly alarmed when he heard of the house being spied on after dark.

"That settles it!" he declared, thumping his fist on the table. "I'll call Chief Collig in the morning and ask him to provide round-the-clock police protection when I'm not home!"

Because of Kerric being nabbed in the Pine Barrens, Mr. Hardy said he also believed that Diablo's gang might have their hideout there. "A spot near the coast would be an ideal base for smuggling, and of course the wilderness would give them perfect cover. So when I read in the paper that you might go to the Pine Barrens, I decided to risk coming home after dark."

"We *are* going, Dad," Frank told him. "Matter of fact, we were planning to leave tomorrow."

"In that case, keep your eyes and ears open. See if you can spot any signs that the gang is operating in that area."

"Will do," Frank and Joe promised.

Next day the five boys headed for the New Jersey timberland. Tony and Chet rode in Biff Hooper's van, which was loaded with most of the camping gear, while Frank and Joe led the way in their yellow sports sedan.

The sky was sunny and cloudless as they sped southward along the Garden State Parkway. Nearing the northern fringe of the Pine Barrens, they turned inland and soon found themselves in a vast, sandy forest world of evergreens stretching away in all directions as far as the eye could reach.

"Wow!" Joe murmured in an awed voice. "Who'd expect a wilderness like this so close to New York City!"

The silence and loneliness were impressive, compared to the busy highway they had just left behind. The only visible landmarks in the piney sea were an occasional distant tower, rising above the treetops.

After passing through the little town of Chatsworth, known as the capital of the Pine Barrens, the boys turned southward. But after following a zigzagging road for mile after mile, they realized they had lost their way.

The next habitation they came to was a weather-beaten building standing near a cranberry bog that was dammed along the sides with turf. An old pickup truck was parked in front of the building.

Maybe we can get directions here," said Frank,

and pulled off the road. Biff's van stopped behind the Hardys' car.

As the boys got out to stretch their legs, a sun-tanned, white-haired man in shirtsleeves emerged from the building to greet them.

"Can I help you fellas?" he inquired, a friendly grin crinkling his face.

"We'd sure appreciate it," Frank said. "We were heading for Cedar Knob, but we've lost our way."

"Just keep on the road you're going for about three more miles, then turn left at the next dirt lane you come to. You can't miss it."

"Thanks." Frank took out the snapshot of Rupert Price. "By the way," he added, "we were told this fellow might be living in the Pine Barrens, and if he is, we'd like to find him. Have you ever seen him?"

The white-haired man took one look at the snapshot. His grin faded. "Nope," he said, and turning on his heel, went back into the building. The door slammed shut behind him.

"Sufferin' snakes!" Chet said. "What got into him all of a sudden?"

"Good question," Frank murmured thoughtfully. "Maybe strangers are only allowed to ask directions. Get any nosier, and the natives clam up!"

Driving on, the boys reached their destination with no further trouble. Cedar Knob proved to be a wooded hill overlooking a crystal-clear lake. Prowling around to pick a campsite, the youths discovered the moldering, wooden remains of what might have been a lean-to.

"Wow!" Joe exclaimed. "This might have been the spot where Jem Taggart's gang took shelter in bad weather!"

The five boys set about unloading their gear from the van and pitched their tents. Later they heard a vehicle approaching. It was an old pickup truck. As the driver slowed and waved, they strolled down the slope to chat with him.

"Gonna camp here a spell?" he inquired.

"Sure are," Biff said. "Looks like we picked a great spot for it, doesn't it?"

"Mighty pretty." With a smile, the man added, "Just don't go startin' any forest fires!"

"Don't worry, we'll be careful," Frank promised. Once again he produced the snapshot from his pocket. "We'd sure like to find this man. Ever seen him, by any chance?"

"Listen, boy!" The man's face hardened. "This is no place for nosy strangers! If ya know what's good for ya, you'll mind your own business!"

8 Weird Booms

The man slammed his truck into gear and drove off without another word. His abrupt, angry departure left the boys startled and momentarily speechless.

"Another nice, friendly Piney," Chet mumbled.

"Something tells me they just don't like outsiders asking questions about their neighbors," Joe guessed.

"That may be the explanation," Frank agreed. "Whatever their reason is, they do get uptight when I show them this picture of Rupert Price."

Since everyone was hungry by now, Frank and Joe volunteered to go shopping, while Chet busied himself with building a stone fireplace and Biff tried the lake for fish. Tony went with the Hardys to acquaint himself with the general "lay of the land."

Twenty minutes of exploratory cruising brought them to a crossroads store. The proprietor, a paunchy, baldheaded man, served them in a friendly fashion and seemed quite talkative, perhaps because there was no one else in the store when they walked in.

"You lads expect to be campin' there on the Knob fer a week or two?" he inquired as he toted up the bill.

"We're not sure how long," Frank replied.

Fishing in his pocket, he felt the devil doll. He set it out on the counter and asked, "Got any idea what that's supposed to be?"

"Sure have." The storekeeper chuckled. "That's the Jersey Devil!"

The boys were thunderstruck by this reply.

"The what?" Joe echoed.

"The Jersey Devil."

"What's that?" Tony asked.

"Well now, that's a long story, young fella." The storekeeper hooked his thumbs behind his suspenders and grinned, pleased to have such an attentive audience. "In fact, you might say it's two or three different stories, dependin' on which one you believe."

"Which one do *you* believe?" said Frank.

"Well, the usual version is that a woman livin' in

these parts, named Mother Leeds, had twelve children—all of 'em normal, human-type kids—but when it turned out another one was on the way, somehow a curse got laid on it. And on account of that curse, her thirteenth child turned into this awful-lookin' devil creature with wings, which flew up the chimney."

Frank smiled at the elderly proprietor. "Quite a yarn. Are the other versions more sensible?"

"Not much. Accordin' to one, the mother got cursed by a gypsy because she wouldn't give him any food. And another story claims the curse was laid by a preacher who'd been mistreated somehow."

The storekeeper paused to tamp a pinch of snuff beneath his lower lip. "Mind you, all these yarns go back to the 1700s, when folks were a lot more superstitious than they are now. But that don't mean the critter itself is just moonshine. Wherever it came from, the thing's been seen by all sorts of witnesses, and there are people right today in these woods who'll swear the Jersey Devil really exists!"

During the past two hundred years or more, the storekeeper related, there were reports of the creature being seen all over South Jersey. It was said to devour livestock and even attack people.

"But the biggest scare," he continued, "came in

1909 when hundreds of people in at least thirty different towns reported seein' the critter in the same week. Some of the witnesses were policemen, and over near Camden a whole trolley car full of passengers saw it flappin' around."

The boys listened attentively, fascinated by the colorful local folklore.

"It sure doesn't sound like a joke when you tell it like that," Tony remarked. "Has the thing been seen in recent years?"

"Yep. Lots of times. Folks have reported hearin' it screech or seein' its tracks, and not too long ago a farmer had a whole flock of ducks and geese mauled by some sort of weird critter. He called a cop, who found strange tracks leading off into the woods."

The three Bayporters learned that the best guess as to the real nature of the Jersey Devil was that it might be a sand hill crane. But privately Frank and Joe suspected that the legend would persist for at least another two hundred years and would no doubt grow with every telling.

In any case, the Hardys were more interested in learning where the tiny plastic devil figure might have come from. But to this question, the store-keeper could offer no answers.

"I'll tell you one fella, though, who made up an image of the Jersey Devil," he went on, "and that was old Jem Taggart."

"You mean the Outlaw of the Pine Barrens?" Joe queried in surprise.

"Yep, only his wasn't any itty-bitty doll like this. It was a great big metal figure forged out of bog iron. He hung it up in a tree near Cedar Knob to scare folks away from his gang's hideout."

"What happened to it?" Frank asked.

"Dunno. It disappeared a while back. Probably got carted off by tourists for a souvenir."

Despite his willingness to talk about the Jersey Devil, however, the storekeeper proved as close-mouthed as any of the other Pineys when shown the snapshot of Rupert Price. He frowned and shook his head, then turned his back on the boys and stalked off into the back room of the store.

Returning to camp, the trio were greeted by Chet and Biff with an air of excitement.

"Wait'll you see what I found!" their chubby pal announced.

He led them to the remains of the robber gang's old lean-to and pointed to a carved inscription. The letters were barely legible in the dank, rotting wood but could still be made out: FISHHOOK X.

"Wow!" Joe exclaimed. "That word 'fishhook' also occurs in Jem Taggart's letter!"

The Hardys got out the letter, which had been packed with their camping gear, to show their three friends. Biff's eyes widened as he read the sentence in question: BURIED SILVER UNDER HIM FISHHOOK TEN PACES NORTH AS CROW FLIES.

"Hey!" he blurted. "Does that mean the treasure may be buried right around here somewhere?" The three boys thoughtfully studied the inscription.

Frank shook his head regretfully. "Can't be," he reasoned. "The way it's written, Jem sent this letter to two other gang members who were here at Cedar Knob, saying he wants them to come and join him. Which means he must have stashed the silver someplace else."

After supper, as the shadows lengthened among the evergreens, they sat around talking over the campfire. Both Chet and Biff were keenly interested in hearing about the Jersey Devil.

"That's the wildest yarn I've heard in a long

time!" Biff commented with a chuckle. "I guess some people will fall for anything."

"What's so strange about that?" Chet replied uneasily. "I bet if you heard weird screeches out in the woods after dark, you'd start believing in the Jersey Devil, too!"

That night, the Hardys were awakened in their tent by an odd, booming sound. As Joe strained his ears, it came again suddenly: *Boooom!*

"Did you hear that?" he muttered to Frank.

"Sure did!"

The brothers emerged cautiously to look around. In the glow from the dying embers of the campfire, they saw Chet also peering nervously from his tent.

"Y-y-you guys heard it, too?" he quavered.

The Hardys nodded, listening alertly.

"I've heard it about half a dozen times," Chet babbled. "How can anyone get to sleep with noises like that going on? No wonder the Pineys talk about devil monsters in these woods!"

Frank got his flashlight and was about to start exploring for signs of any animal or human intruder on the wooded hillside when a bird came diving out of the darkness straight toward their camp. As it spread its wings to pull out of the dive, another *boooom!* resounded in the night air!

Joe burst out laughing in relief. "It's a night-hawk!"

"Diving for insects," Frank added. "We can all go back to sleep, Chet, with nothing to fear."

The stout boy snorted grumpily. "The Federal Aviation Agency should cite those things for causing sonic booms!"

Next morning, as the boys were cooking breakfast, a motorcycle rider stopped and greeted them with a friendly wave. "Mornin'!" he called out and slowed to a halt.

The boys talked to him for a while, then Frank pulled out the snapshot of Rupert Price. The young detectives were amazed when the man's manner did not change.

"Sure, I know that guy," he admitted promptly. "I can take you right to him!"

9 Grave Evidence

The stranger's response was so unexpected that at first the Hardys wondered if he might be joking or making fun of them.

"Are you serious?" Frank asked sharply.

"'Course I'm serious," the man retorted. "Why should I lie to you?"

The Hardys studied him for a moment before replying. He was rather thin and bony in build, with a freckled face and sparse, sandy hair. His expression seemed open and friendly.

"I guess we just weren't expecting such a stroke of luck." Joe grinned. "Got time for a cup of coffee?"

"You bet!"

"Great. We haven't had breakfast yet, but if you can wait for a few minutes and then take us to the man we're looking for, we'll sure appreciate it."

Frank, Joe, Tony, and Biff bolted down their food, excited at the prospect of meeting Rupert Price and hearing his story. They were eager to see his reaction to the news that he was no longer wanted by the law. Chet agreed to stay and watch the camp while the others accompanied the motorcyclist.

The boys piled into the Hardys' car and followed the man, who led them on a zigzag route, over several unpaved roads and rutted forest trails, to an ancient, weather-beaten cabin.

"Doesn't look like anyone lives here," Frank remarked as the procession came to a stop and the boys got out.

"You're right, no one does," the thin man said grimly. "Not any more, anyhow."

Without another word, he led them to a shallow, oblong mound at the edge of the clearing. It was overgrown with weeds and wildflowers, but there was no doubt that they were looking at a grave, as evidenced by a wooden cross stuck in the ground at one end. The cross bore a crudely carved inscription, RUPERT PRICE, with a date underneath the name.

"He came down with pneumonia and died last winter," their guide explained.

All four boys were saddened by Rupert's fate. They had been looking forward to greeting him with the news of his vindication.

"Is that where he had been living?" Frank inquired with a frown, gesturing toward the cabin.

"Yup, lived there quite a few years."

The thin, sandy-haired man walked with them to the weather-beaten shack. Inside, it was divided into two rooms, both largely empty now, except for such items as a rusty stove, a sagging metal bedstead, and a battered, overturned table with one leg off.

The only traces of Price's occupancy were a threadbare, once-white towel stenciled with the name R. E. PRICE, USN; a similarly stenciled, cracked plastic toilet case now containing only a well-worn toothbrush and the twisted remnant of a tube of shaving cream; and a yellowing snapshot tacked up on one wall. The photo showed Price in a navy uniform with a shipmate in some Oriental city, presumably while on liberty in port during a Pacific cruise.

"Is this all he left?" Joe asked.

Their guide shrugged. "It's all that's left *now*. I guess folks who come by have helped themselves to anything they figured they could use. He never did have much, far as I know."

The boys thanked him for his help and returned to camp.

Chet Morton's moonface sagged sympathetically when he heard the news. "Too bad. You guys better have one of my sassafras milkshakes to cheer you up."

"What's that? Don't tell me you're off on another one of your nutty fads," Tony said suspiciously.

"Fad my eye!" Chet replied. "Nature's full of tasty tidbits, if you're a real woodsman who knows how to live off the wilderness."

The others grinned warily. But after sampling Chet's milkshakes, they all drank down the concoction with hearty smacks of appreciation.

"Not bad, Chet!" Frank said. "But I'm not so sure we need cheering up."

"How come? You mean you halfway expected Price might be dead by now?"

"Not really. I'm not convinced he *is* dead!"

The chubby youth stared in puzzled surprise. "But you just told me you saw his grave!"

"We saw *a* grave, or something that looked like a grave," Frank replied. "But that doesn't prove Rupert Price is buried there."

"Wasn't there a wooden cross with his name on it?"

"Yes. But I've a hunch that was stuck there later, just to mislead us. The grave was sunken in and pretty overgrown with grass and weeds, as if it had been there for a while. But the marker didn't look nearly that old. The wood was all weather-beaten, but that doesn't prove anything. It could have been taken from somewhere else. What counts was the lettering on it, and that looked to me as if it had been newly carved."

Both Tony and Biff had been frowning thoughtfully as they listened to the conversation, and Tony nodded in agreement. "Yeah, now that you mention it, I noticed that, too."

"The cabin didn't look as if it had been lived in very recently, either," Frank pointed out. "If you ask me, it hasn't been lived in for a lot longer than just last winter."

"That figures," Biff said.

"Another thing," Frank said, "was that broken table leg. If that had happened while Rupert Price was there, he'd have fixed it. But it looked as if it had rotted off a long time ago, while the cabin was vacant."

"So what are we going to do about it?" Biff asked.

"I vote we go back for another look," Joe said, "without our helpful friend on the motorcycle watching us."

The boys were eager to accompany the Hardys

and probe deeper into the mystery, but it was decided that Biff should stay behind this time to guard the camp.

The four Bayporters retraced the route over which the motorcyclist had led them. Presently they stopped at the tumbledown shack and got out.

"First, let's examine the grave again," Frank suggested, "and see if we can spot any clues."

"Look here," Joe pointed out when they stood before the wooden cross. "The hole's at least a quarter of an inch bigger than the marker!"

"Couldn't that just be due to the marker sagging or getting blown over a bit by the wind?" said Chet.

"Maybe—only this marker isn't sagging. It's been pounded down hard, yet there's extra room in the hole on each side of it."

Joe glanced at his brother. "You mean as if this were a new marker, and the original were bigger?"

"Right. Which brings up another point. If the marker had been here very long, that hollow space would probably have filled in, just with windblown particles or by gradual shifting of the soil."

As he spoke, Frank began tugging at the wooden cross and soon pulled it up enough to expose the lower part that had previously been hidden from view. Then he brushed away bits of the sandy soil still clinging to the wood.

"No difference in weathering, above and below ground," Joe exclaimed. "I'd say that proves this marker's just been stuck in recently."

Moments later, they heard a triumphant cry from Tony Prito. He had poked about in the underbrush after hearing Frank's deductions about the grave marker.

"Look what I found!" Tony announced, holding up another wooden cross.

As he brought it over to show the others, they saw that the name on it was "Ezekiel King" and the carved burial date was more than ten years before Rupert Price's alleged death! Moreover, the upright member of this cross was about a quarter of an inch wider than that of the present marker, so it would have fitted the hole perfectly.

The wood of the newly found cross was also whiter, and even though its inscription showed obvious signs of weathering, the letters were still sharply visible.

"It's made from heart of pine," said Frank. "I remember Dad telling me about this stuff once. It never rots."

Joe suddenly clutched his brother's arm and hissed, "Sh!"

There was a rustling noise from among the trees on their right.

"Someone's spying on us!" Chet whispered.

His legs went into action as he ran in the direction of the sound. The other boys followed. They could hear footsteps now, pounding away in the distance, and caught a fleeting glimpse of a running figure before he was lost to view among the densely clustering pines.

"Spread out!" Frank shouted to his companions.

They did so, hoping to trap the fugitive if he tried to veer sharply to shake them off. Before they could overtake him, however, the thunderous *vroom!* of a motorcycle engine echoed through the woods. The sound of the bike soon dwindled in the distance.

"Gnats!" Joe growled, clenching his fists in angry frustration. "I'll bet it was that skinny, sandy-haired guy who tried to con us!"

"Probably," Frank agreed. "But never mind. The guy just outsmarted himself."

"How do you mean?" said Tony.

"He must've planted that new grave marker to convince us Rupert Price was dead. But now that we know it's phony, I'd say it's a safe bet Rupert Price is still alive."

"And probably hiding out in these woods," Joe reasoned.

Considerably heartened, the four Bayporters drove back to camp. As they climbed out of the car, they heard a moaning sound coming from one of the tents.

"Something's wrong with Biff!" exclaimed Frank.

They ran to his tent and found their friend sprawled on his sleeping bag, rolling his eyes and clutching his midriff.

"Biff, what's the matter?" Joe cried.

"I picked some wild grapes and ate them," Biff explained between moans, "but they must have been rotten. They tasted awful! I couldn't even keep them down!"

"Sure they were grapes?" Frank asked.

"Well, they *looked* like grapes. What else could they be?"

"Where are they growing?"

After listening to Biff's reply, Frank went off to investigate. He soon came back, holding a cluster of dark, purplish-black fruit. "Is this what you ate?"

Biff nodded, his cheeks pale and sickly hued.

"No wonder! These aren't grapes. We have some climbing our back fence. Aunt Gertrude calls them moonseed." Frank squeezed one of the fruits to show its crescent-shaped pit and added, "You're lucky you didn't keep the stuff down. You could've poisoned yourself!" Quickly, he boiled some water and gave Biff a mug of tea to soothe his stomach.

Later, after attending to various camp chores, the

Hardys pored over several books on the Pine Barrens which they had brought along, and studied their case notes.

Suddenly, Joe snapped his fingers and exclaimed, "Hey, Frank! I have an idea!"

10 Danger Trail

Frank looked up. "I'm all ears. Let's hear your idea."

"It concerns that crook named Kerric that Dad told us about," Joe said.

"The one who was picked up in the Pine Barrens with the devil doll in his pocket?"

"Right. Remember how it happened?"

"Sure. Dad said he walked up to a gas station, and there was a state trooper who recognized and arrested him."

Joe nodded. "Now why do you suppose Kerric would have been *walking* to a gas station down here in the boondocks?"

Frank hesitated. "Maybe he ran out of gas—or his car broke down."

"Right!" Joe burst out. "And if he did—or it did—then maybe his car is still standing where he left it."

"Wow!" Frank's eyes lit up with excitement as his brother's words sank in. "I'd say that's worth checking out! If the car *is* still there, it may contain an important clue!"

"Just what I'm thinking. But first we'll have to find out where the gas station is located."

"Dad can probably tell us. Let's call him on the radio."

Fenton Hardy soon responded to the transmission. He showed immediate interest on hearing Joe's idea. "Good thinking, Son. In an area as isolated as the Pine Barrens, a car could easily stand by the road for several weeks before anyone reported it to the police. By all means, have a look."

Luckily, the detective was able to give his sons precise directions, which enabled them to locate the gas station on their road map. He also described Kerric, in case they had to question anyone about the crook's movements.

Snores were now coming from Chet's tent, while Biff and Tony busily assembled a metal detector. They had rented it in Bayport and planned to run it over the area around the camp in order to check for signs of hidden treasure.

After telling them where they were going, the Hardys headed southwest from Cedar Knob.

It was late afternoon when they finally reached the gas station. Frank pulled in and asked the mechanic attending the pumps to fill their tank. Afterward, the boys bought three sodas from the soft drink machine, offered one to the mechanic, and engaged him in friendly conversation.

"I hear some crook the FBI was after got picked up at your place," Frank remarked casually.

"Yup. I saw it happen," the mechanic replied.

"Any fireworks?" Joe inquired.

"Nope. A state trooper was here getting a busted fan belt replaced on his patrol car. He was in plain clothes, and his car was up on the lift in the garage, so the guy didn't realize he was walking right into the clutches of the law. The trooper had a gun on him before he even knew he'd been spotted!"

"What was he doing down in the Pine Barrens?"

"Search me." The mechanic pointed down the highway to the left. "He just came hiking along the road, and two minutes later he was wearing handcuffs!"

The Hardys finished their drinks and drove off in the direction that the mechanic had indicated. They stopped a short distance from the service station and got out of the car.

"Let's split up and each take one side of the road," Frank suggested. "We'll have to proceed slowly because I have a feeling Kerric hid his car well. Otherwise the authorities would have found it."

Joe nodded. "I'll take the right, you take the left."

Carefully, the young detectives worked their way through the underbrush and trees, stirring up gnats and mosquitoes. I hope we find this car before I get eaten up alive, Joe thought, swatting a bug on his forehead.

Frank lost his footing a couple of times and stumbled, barely avoiding a fall. His arm scraped against the bark of a tree and tore the skin. But he plodded on determinedly.

After a half hour of searching, Joe suddenly called out, "Frank!" He ran through the brush to the road, yelling Frank's name a few more times. Finally he was near enough for his brother to hear him.

"Did you find anything?" Frank exclaimed, fighting his way through the heavily wooded area.

"I sure did. Come over here!"

It took a few moments for Frank to scramble over to Joe's side. When he reached his brother, he whooped with joy.

A car had rolled down the sandy shoulder from

the blacktop highway and come to a stop among the pine trees. It was so well concealed that it could only be seen from a vantage point between two bushy evergreens.

"This could be it, Joe!" Frank cried.

"I sure hope so," his brother replied. "I'm exhausted from looking for it!"

The boys examined their find, an expensive-looking, gunmetal-gray two-door sedan. It was in such a lonely spot that evidently the driver had not thought it necessary to lock up. This also seemed to indicate that he had expected to return soon.

A buzz sounded as Joe opened the door, and he noticed the key had been left in the ignition. Then he saw a piece of paper lying on the passenger side of the front seat.

"Hey, look at this, Frank!" he blurted, snatching it up. The paper bore a rough sketch map in pencil with the words:

KERRIC—FOLLOW THIS ROUTE.

"Jumpin' catfish! We really struck gold!" his brother murmured.

On the back seat was a portable, battery-powered ultraviolet sunlamp. The only other item of interest was a matchbook lying on the dashboard bearing an advertisement for a restaurant called the Pirate's Tavern, together with a diagram showing its highway position on the edge of the Pine Barrens near the coast.

The Hardys examined the paper closely for several moments before Frank muttered, "It shows the road we're on, Joe. It even has the gas station marked back there."

"You're right," Joe said, "and this looks like some kind of road about a mile ahead where he was supposed to turn off. I bet Kerric was on his way there when his car conked out on him!"

"The big question is, where would this route have taken him?"

Joe grinned. "There's one way to find out!"

Twenty minutes later, their yellow sports sedan was tooling down the road toward the turnoff. This proved to be little more than a rough, rutted track leading in among the pines. The boys followed it cautiously, jouncing up and down even though the car was moving at a very slow speed.

"Wow! Let's hope our springs hold out!" Joe said.

By now, the sun had sunk behind a cloud bank in the west, and the lengthening shadows, added to the natural forest gloom, gave the woods a sinister atmosphere. Twilight was falling fast as they reached a point where the trail became too narrow and brushy for the car to proceed.

"Now what?" Joe muttered in a hollow voice.

Frank had a sudden hunch. He got out, took the

sunlamp from the back seat, switched it on, and shone it all around. Both boys gasped as they saw a blaze mark glow into view on a nearby tree.

"Must be painted with fluorescent dye!" Joe exclaimed.

"And it points to the right," Frank added.

Joe got out of the car to join his brother, and the two boys pressed on through the deepening darkness, guided by other blaze marks every ten yards or so.

The trail wound on through the forest. Frank swung the sunlamp back and forth, so that its ultraviolet rays would miss none of the markers.

Suddenly, both boys stopped short in shock. Ahead of them, a ghastly glowing figure had just materialized out of the darkness.

"It's the Jersey Devil!" Joe cried out.

11 Colonial Ghost

For an instant, the Hardys were frozen with fright.
The grotesque, glowing creature with its outspread
bat wings looked as if it were about to fly straight
down and attack them!

Then Frank sighed with relief. "Relax! That
thing's not real, Joe!"

"You're right," his brother murmured huskily.
"It's not moving. But what is it?"

Frank was equally puzzled at first. But as he
stepped forward and nerved himself to touch the
scary-looking image, the answer suddenly clicked in
his memory. "I'll tell you what it is!" he exclaimed.
"It's that devil figure made out of bog iron that the

storekeeper told us about! The one that Jem Taggart's gang used to frighten away snoopers!"

"You're right again," Joe concurred as he, too, fingered the metallic monster. "What's it doing here, though?"

"Good question." Frank brooded a moment before adding, "One thing's certain. Taggart's gang never coated it with fluorescent paint!"

"That's for sure. They didn't even have such a thing in those days. I'd say it's Diablo's gang who supplied the fluorescent touch, wouldn't you? At least that's how it looks, if we assume they're the ones who blazed that trail through the woods with all those fluorescent tree markings."

The older Hardy boy nodded. "That has to be the explanation. Which means they must also be the ones who moved the thing here from Cedar Knob."

But why? Neither boy could offer a convincing answer.

Joe glanced about uneasily. "It'll be pitch dark soon, Frank. Maybe we'd better not hang around here."

"I second the motion."

Only the glowing marks on the tree trunks enabled the Hardys to find their way back to the point where the weird trail began. Frank started the car and shifted into reverse. Joe guided him backward along the rutted track until they came to a place where there was enough room between the trees to turn the car around.

During the long drive back to Cedar Knob, the Hardys discussed the mystery and talked over their latest discovery. But the conversation trailed off as both boys became more aware of the gnawing hollow between their ribs due to lack of food.

"Let's hope the gang's whipped up something good for supper," Frank muttered as they whizzed along the road.

"You said it. And if they did, let's also hope that Chet hasn't gobbled it all up already," Joe quipped wryly.

An unpleasant disappointment was in store. As the Hardys pulled up at the edge of camp and got out, the expressions on the faces of their three friends who came to meet them was a plain announcement of bad news.

"Hey, what's wrong?" Joe demanded.

"Plenty!" Chet blurted. "Some dirty crook swiped all our chow!"

"We were out searching for treasure with the metal detector," Tony related. "We got so engrossed we didn't get back to camp till twilight. Then, when we started to get supper, we suddenly discovered there was no food!"

"Somebody raided the camp while we were gone and cleaned us out completely!" Biff added, with a look of angry exasperation.

"Sure it was a human thief?" Frank asked.

"You can bet your life it was no raccoon, if that's what you're thinking!" Biff retorted. "Whoever did it even opened our ice chest and pinched our milk cartons and bottles of soda! Boy, if I could get my hands on that dirty sneak, I'd wring his neck!"

"Me, too! I'm starving!" Chet grumbled.

"Any clues?" Frank pursued.

"We're stepping on most of them," Tony said, "if you can call them clues." He shone his flashlight at the sandy soil around the open door of Biff's van, where the supplies had been kept. "See those brush marks?"

The Hardys nodded glumly. "He must've used a pine bough to brush away his footprints," Frank declared. "But I'll see if I can get some fingerprints off the van. We can have them checked out later."

He managed to lift two clear prints, and when he was finished, Biff said, "Who do you suppose did it?"

Frank's face was serious as he shrugged. "It could have been El Diablo's gang—which may mean we're closer to them than we realized. On the other hand, it could also have been our friendly treasure-hunting competitor, Ambrose Verrill."

"For that matter," said Joe, "it could even have been that skinny guy on the motorcycle who tried to trick us into believing Rupert Price was dead. Since that didn't work, maybe now he's going to try and *starve* us out!"

"Yeah, that sure figures," Tony Prito said.

"Never mind all the fancy theories," Chet cut in plaintively. "The important thing is, what're we going to do for supper tonight?"

Frank grinned and threw an arm around the chunky youth's shoulder. "Relax, pal—there's more food where that stolen grub came from. That general store's probably still open."

"By the way," Frank added as he and his brother headed toward their car, "did you guys have any luck with the metal detector?"

"We got a few buzzes," Biff reported, "but they turned out to be empty cans or old rusty auto parts—junk like that."

"Too bad. At least we've learned a lesson, though. From now on, we'd better never leave the camp without someone to guard it."

"You said it!"

Luckily, when the Hardys reached the general store, its windows were still lit. Inside, the bald, paunchy proprietor was engaged in an after-hours, yarn-spinning conversation with several friends.

"You fellas must have right hearty appetites!" he

remarked with a chuckle, as the boys replenished the camp's supplies. "Weren't you in here just yesterday, stockin' up on vittles?"

Frank was about to report the robbery, but after a quick glance at Joe, he decided against it. He feared that the storekeeper and his cronies might take offense at the idea of outsiders implying a local Piney might be responsible. Instead, he merely replied, "We did, but we had an accident and lost some. By the way, we had a visitor this morning. We'd like to look him up again if we could find him, but we forgot to get his name."

"What'd he look like, Son?"

"Sandy hair, freckles, sort of thin and bony. He was riding a motorcycle."

"Oh, that musta been Willard Bosley," spoke up one of the men who were lounging in the store.

"Any idea where we can find him?" Joe asked. "We're camping on Cedar Knob."

"Sure, Willard lives about four, five miles southwest of there." The man proceeded to give the Hardys detailed directions for finding Bosley's cabin.

He had barely finished speaking when the door burst open and a wild-eyed man in a plaid flannel shirt and worn corduroy pants rushed into the store.

"What in tarnation's wrong with you, Pete?" the

storekeeper asked. "You look like y' just seen a ghost!"

"Right the first time!" the newcomer blurted excitedly. "That's exactly what I saw!"

His words and manner brought the group lounging around the counter to rapt attention.

"Are you kiddin'?" one of the men asked.

"Naw, I'm not kiddin'!" Pete replied. "And it wasn't just *any* ghost—it was *Jem Taggart's ghost!*"

The startling announcement aroused the boys' curiosity.

"Someone's pulling your leg, Pete," another man joked. "What'd he do—sneak up behind you and yell *boo!* in your ear?"

"Listen, wise guy!" Pete flared back. "This was no joke—and it was no live man, either!"

"How d'you know?"

" 'Cause he was all dressed up in old-time Colonial duds, that's how—includin' knee britches! And his face was dead white! If that wasn't a ghost, I'll eat your hat!"

The store loungers were taken aback by these unexpected details. But most of them still seemed to think Pete's imagination was running away with him. The Hardys listened to the wisecracks and speculation that continued for a while longer, then quickly paid their bill and left.

"Wow! What do you make of *that* story?" Joe asked his brother as they loaded the supplies into their car.

"Beats me," Frank said. "But I've got a hunch it may be connected to this mystery we're trying to solve."

Joe agreed. Back at camp, their three friends listened avidly to Frank and Joe's account of the strange incident. Chet Morton looked a trifle uneasy, but his nervousness soon gave way to a hearty appetite as the smell of baked beans, beef stew, and roasting potatoes filled the night air.

After they had finished clearing away the remains of supper and washed up the cooking utensils, the five boys retired to their tents and sleeping bags. Some time later Frank and Joe were awakened from a deep slumber by eerie wailing noises.

"That's no nighthawk!" Joe exclaimed.

"You can say that again," Frank agreed, squirming out of his sleeping bag.

Flashlights in hand, the boys hurried outside. Tony had already emerged from the tent he shared with Biff, and the other two appeared moments later, pulling on their jeans. All were tense and wide-eyed as they listened to the spooky wails.

"They're coming from there," Tony said, pointing westward along the shore of the lake.

"Could be that same joker who raided our camp!" Joe conjectured.

"Yes. Let me at him!" growled Biff, casting about for a stout stick. "If it *is* him, he'd better get ready to do some fast talking!"

Chet was as eager for revenge as the others.

"Might be a good idea if we all took sticks," Frank suggested. "Whoever he is, he could be a bit nutty—and he may have a mean streak!"

The boys started down the hillside and fanned out, hoping to surround their tormentor. In the moonlit darkness, with brush bordering the lake, they were soon lost to each other's view. But a sudden scream from Chet brought Frank, Joe, and Tony rushing to his side.

"What's up, Chet?" Joe exclaimed.

"Th-th-the ghost!" stuttered the fat boy.

"*What* ghost?" Frank demanded sharply.

"*Jem Taggart's ghost!* The one that guy at the store was telling you about—with knee britches and all! And that dead white face! I saw him right over there through the trees!"

Chet's hand shook as he pointed. His three listeners exchanged startled looks, hardly knowing what to make of his story.

Next moment, another yell split the darkness!

"Hey, that's Biff!" cried Frank. "Something's *really* wrong!"

12 Pirate's Tavern

The four boys started back to camp on the run.
Hearts thudding, they pounded up the hillside,
trampling their way through the heavy undergrowth.

Frank's flashlight picked out Biff's face in the
darkness. He looked both angry and rattled.

"What's going on?" Frank asked.

"We've been had, that's what!"

"How come?" Tony blurted.

"When we were fanned out in the woods, all of a
sudden I remembered what Frank said about never
leaving the camp unguarded. So I came back to
keep an eye on things, and that's what I found!"

Frank swung his flashlight in the direction Biff

was pointing. The yellow beam settled on the van. Its door was hanging open again. The ice chest had been lifted out, and various other items lay scattered on the ground.

"We've been raided again!" Chet moaned.

"Was anything taken?" Joe inquired as the boys hurried to inspect the van more closely.

Biff shrugged. "I don't think so, but I'm not sure yet. I've a hunch whoever it was searched our tents first. Then he was poking around in the van. When he heard me coming back, he scrammed."

After a hasty check, the Hardys and their friends concluded that nothing was missing. Frank, however, was glad that he had been carrying the devil doll with him in the pocket of his jeans. Also, much to his and Joe's relief, the raider had not taken the ultraviolet sunlamp and other items that the two brothers had removed from Kerric's abandoned car in order to safeguard them until they could be turned over to the proper authorities.

"Looks to me like our midnight visitor didn't have time to go through *our* car," Joe commented.

Frank nodded glumly. "That's one consolation, I guess. But I could kick myself for not realizing those spooky wails were just a trick to lure us away from camp."

"Listen! That ghost I saw was no trick!" Chet declared. "It was there, plain as anything!"

111

"What ghost?" Biff asked.

"Jem Taggart's ghost!" Chet described the white-faced figure in Colonial costume in great detail.

"What makes you so sure that wasn't part of the trick?" Tony demanded. "Somebody could've dressed up like that just to make the wailing seem even more spooky."

"Why would they go to all that trouble?" Chet retorted. "The wailing noises worked all by themselves, didn't they? They were enough to decoy us out in the woods. Besides, where would anyone get clothes like that on short notice?"

"Chet's got a point there," Frank agreed. "I'm not saying he saw a real ghost, mind you, but whatever it was—or whoever it was—may not have had anything to do with the raid on our camp."

The boys discussed the night's events for a while longer. Finally, they went back to their tents, and once again the camp was wrapped in silence as they drifted off to sleep.

Next morning, following the directions they had obtained from the Piney at the general store, the Hardys drove to Willard Bosley's house. This proved to be a shingle shack covered with peeling tar paper. Nearby lay two rusting, wheelless cars, a litter of cranberry boxes, and a stack of cordwood. The owner's motorcycle was leaning against the front wall of the shack.

As the Hardys' car jounced up the rutted path and drew to a halt, Bosley himself and a little girl appeared in the doorway to see who was coming. The girl, who was about six years old and evidently his daughter, was barefoot and had shimmering reddish-gold hair. Clutching a wooden doll in one arm, she skipped out eagerly, openly admiring the sleek and shiny vehicle.

"Your car is the prettiest I've ever seen!"

"Well, you're pretty, too, honey." Frank smiled. "What's your name?"

"Della," the little girl replied, and added gravely, "I probably look okay now, but last spring I was real sick and I must'a looked awful!"

"No kidding?" Joe said sympathetically. "What was the matter?"

"Well, I don't know exactly, but it was pretty bad. Daddy thought I was never gonna get well, and maybe I never would've except for—"

"That'll be enough out of you, Della," her father interrupted, kindly but firmly. "These fellas didn't come here t' hear about your health."

The thin, sandy-haired Piney had been hanging back in the doorway with a rather sullen air, as if reluctant to face the two boys after what had happened the day before. But now he stepped outside defiantly and flung an arm around his daughter's shoulders, drawing her close to him.

Since he showed no sign of going off to work, Frank and Joe assumed that Bosley must be an odd-job laborer, who followed the regular Pine Barrens work cycle they had read about—gathering sphagnum moss in the spring, picking blueberries in the summer and cranberries in the fall, and then chopping wood during the cold winter months.

Frank hesitated before speaking, not quite sure how to begin. "Mr. Bosley," he said finally, "my brother and I are anxious to find Rupert Price. We have some important news to tell him."

"I've already told you he's dead," Willard Bosley responded in a curt voice.

"I know that's what you said." Frank hesitated again uncomfortably, not wanting to accuse Bosley of lying. "But we're pretty sure—well, anyhow, we think you may be mistaken. We have a hunch he may still be hiding out because he thinks the law is after him."

"But he doesn't have to worry about that any more," Joe said. "He was cleared of that murder charge a long time ago."

"Right," Frank went on. "And now he's inherited a lot of money from his uncle, and his Cousin Ogden's trying to find him, because if he doesn't come forward to claim his inheritance, he'll lose out on his share of the money."

Bosley's freckled face had taken on a frown while

the boys were speaking. He stared at them intently for a moment, but finally shook his head. "I'm sorry, but you two have got it all wrong. You can believe whatever you like, but I'm telling you Rupert Price died of pneumonia last winter."

Joe started to argue, pointing out that the grave Bosley had shown them was obviously not that recent. But Frank cut his brother short, realizing they had no way of forcing Bosley to stop covering up for the missing man.

"We're telling you the truth about that inheritance," the older Hardy boy declared bluntly. "And if you're a real friend of Rupert Price, or know any friend of his, I hope you'll see that he gets the news."

Turning to his brother, Frank added, "Come on, Joe. Let's go."

As they drove off, Joe waved to little Della Bosley. In the rearview mirror, Frank saw her father staring after them with a troubled expression.

"What's your guess?" Joe asked his brother. "Was he lying to us?"

"He doesn't trust us, that's for sure," Frank replied. "I'd be willing to bet he's trying to protect Rupert Price."

'Wonder if he'll pass on the news like you asked?"

Frank shrugged. "Guess we'll just have to wait and see."

Arriving back at camp, the Hardys announced their intention of checking out the Pirate's Tavern, the restaurant advertised on the matchbook cover they had found in Kerric's abandoned car. Chet elected to go with them.

They found the place after a lengthy ride. It was a large, white, frame building just off the Garden State Parkway, with a parking lot in front.

The waitress who came to serve them kept staring at Frank and Joe as she took the boys' orders. "Say, aren't you two the Hardy boys?" she blurted.

The brothers nodded. "Guilty as charged," Frank said.

"How'd you guess?" Joe added.

"I saw your picture in the paper," the young woman said brightly. "I thought your faces looked familiar but I couldn't place you. Then I remembered that news story about how you were hunting for treasure here. Did you find it yet?"

"Not even a plugged nickel!" Frank chuckled. Partly to evade further questions on the subject, he asked if she had recently seen a chunky, hoarse-voiced man with bristly black hair, wearing a short-sleeved, tan safari jacket. This was the description of Kerric that Fenton Hardy had given the boys.

"Hey, yes! I do recall someone like that coming in here," the waitress exclaimed, "especially when you mentioned his hoarse voice. The guy sounded like a bullfrog! That was about a week or two ago."

"Anyone with him?" Joe asked.

"No, I think he was alone."

Two men were talking intently in a nearby booth. One paused to unzip a black bag. Frank was startled as he saw him take out a portable sunlamp.

Nudging Joe, Frank drew the waitress's attention to the pair. "Are those fellows regular customers, by any chance?" he murmured.

She shot a quick glance in their direction. She seemed to sense at once that Frank's question was prompted by a mystery case the boys were working on, and the Hardys guessed that she was thrilled at the chance to help out in such an investigation. "I'll need a better look before I know for sure," she replied. "Wait a minute."

The waitress walked back to the kitchen to deliver the boys' order. As she returned, she glanced casually at the two men in the booth, then looked at the Hardys and shook her head.

"Don't think I've ever seen them before," she reported. "From the sneaky way they've got their heads together, it wouldn't surprise me if they were deerjackers."

"Deerjackers?" said Chet. "What's that?"

"Poachers who shoot deer out of season for meat. Often they do it on order for contractors who make a business out of selling venison."

Presently the waitress brought their hamburgers and french fries. As the boys ate, they kept an eye on the two men. After a while, one of them, who had a tanned face and whitish-blond hair, got up from the booth and left.

"I'm going after him," Frank muttered, "to see if I can get his car license number before he drives away."

Joe nodded and watched the man's partner, who had remained seated in the booth. His back was turned to the Bayporters, but as he finished his coffee and glanced idly around the dining room, Chet heard the younger Hardy boy gasp.

"What's the matter, Joe?"

"Take a look at that guy. Isn't that Flat Nose?"

"Hey, I think you're right!"

By this time, Frank had been gone for several minutes. As they waited for him to return, both Joe and Chet began to get worried.

"Wonder what's keeping him?" the chubby youth murmured.

"Maybe we'd better find out!" said Joe, springing to his feet.

Leaving enough money on the table to cover their bill and tip the waitress, the two boys strode off to check on Frank.

A narrow corridor led from the dining room to the small lobby. Halfway along was a turnoff leading to the restrooms and a phone booth. Joe stopped short as he saw a dark-haired figure crumpled inside the booth.

"It's Frank!" he exclaimed.

13 Sun Flashes

Joe and Chet hurried toward the telephone booth. Frank was already stirring back to consciousness as they reached him.

"Wow! What hit me?" he moaned, opening his eyes and getting his bearings.

"I don't know *what* hit you," Joe replied, "but I can make a good guess *who*."

"So can I," Frank muttered wryly. "Something tells me it was that hood I tried to follow." He struggled to his feet and stepped out of the booth, while the other two supported him by the arms until he felt steady enough to stay upright under his own power.

"What happened?" Chet asked.

"What you're probably thinking. By the time I

got across the dining room and into the corridor, the guy was nowhere in sight. I figured he was already out in the parking lot, getting ready to drive off, so I made a dash for the lobby. It never occurred to me that he might be laying in wait for me. When I came past the turnoff—*wham!*—I got conked over the head and was out like a light. After that, I suppose he dragged me into the booth so nobody would spot me before he made his getaway."

Frank gingerly rubbed the sore spot on his head as he spoke.

"Never mind," Joe said tensely. "His buddy's still in the dining room—and he looks like Flat Nose!"

"You mean he *was* there when you two got up."

"Where else would he be?" Chet asked. "I haven't seen him leave while we've been talking to you."

"This isn't the only way out," Frank said.

"You're right!" Joe exclaimed. "If the guy knew he was being followed, they must have spotted us! Flat Nose sure won't sit around waiting to be arrested or tailed!"

The three hurried back into the dining room. Chet groaned irritably as Frank's hunch proved correct. The booth previously occupied by the two suspects was now empty!

"He probably slipped out the back door while we were gone," Joe conjectured. The waitress, who had served the three boys confirmed his guess.

The Hardys and Chet ran out to the parking lot with the slim hope that the men might not have driven off yet, but there was no sign of them. Glumly the trio returned to their car.

"Wait a minute," Frank said suddenly. "Maybe we're passing up a lead."

"Like what?" Joe asked.

"That tow-haired guy I chased took the ultraviolet lamp when he left."

Joe whistled. "Just like Kerric!"

Chet looked from Frank to Joe with a baffled expression and mumbled, "I don't get it."

"Kerric had one of those sunlamps for a certain purpose. We think it had something to do with him coming down here to the Pine Barrens, and also with the fact that he was dodging the law. If so, maybe that bleached-blond creep is a wanted criminal, too!"

"Won't hurt to check on him," Joe added. "You guys stay there. I'll call Sam Radley."

Radley was one of Fenton Hardy's most trusted operatives and had often assisted the sleuth's sons on other mystery cases. Joe hurried to the phone booth in the restaurant and dialed Sam's number.

"Whitish-blond hair, deeply tanned skin, height about five-ten, weight one-seventy," Sam repeated as he jotted down the description Joe had just given him. "Doesn't ring a bell offhand, but I'll see if he has a record."

"Thanks, Sam. If you turn up anything, call us right away on the car radio, please."

"Will do."

Frank and Chet were waiting in the car. "Now what?" asked the stout boy as Joe joined them.

"I think we ought to take a look at the Jersey Devil figure in the woods by daylight," Frank proposed, "especially after seeing another sunlamp."

"Right," Joe agreed.

As they whizzed along the highway en route to the turnoff spot where the blaze-marked trail led deep among the pines, the boys recounted their discovery of the night before for their friends' benefit. Chet was keenly interested. But when they finally reached the turnoff, he made no objection to staying in the car to answer the radio in case Sam Radley transmitted any information.

Frank and Joe, meanwhile, started into the woods on foot. It was not as easy to follow the fluorescent tree markings in the daytime as it had been in the twilight and gathering darkness. However, beyond the point where the rutted trail became too indistinct to follow, tramped underbrush helped guide them in the right direction.

At last, their steps slowed to a halt as they came

in sight of the hanging metal demon figure. Even with the afternoon sun in full view above the treetops, the grotesque, bat-winged, iron monster retained its sinister aspect.

"Charming creature, isn't it?" Frank remarked wryly. "The question is, why did Diablo's gang hang it here?"

Joe looked around thoughtfully. "Maybe for the same reason Jem Taggart's bunch—" His voice broke off with a sudden gasp.

"What's the matter?" Frank asked sharply.

"That tree! Take a look!" Joe pointed to a tall oak nearby.

Metal spikes had been driven into its trunk, apparently as footholds for climbing!

As the boys' gaze followed the trunk upward, they saw a wooden platform or tree house on the upper branches, where the oak's crown reared above the surrounding pines.

"Must be some kind of lookout post!" Frank exclaimed.

Joe was about to climb up, but Frank restrained him. "Hold it! Let's make sure no one's up there, first."

The Hardys moved some distance away and circled about the oak, shading their eyes and peering at the platform from all directions until they were reasonably certain it was unoccupied. Then they scaled up the trunk, spike by spike, with Frank in the lead.

The planking that formed the floor of the platform was enclosed by a rickety wooden railing, with four corner-posts to support a flimsy roof that looked somewhat newer than the rest of the structure. A stout wooden box had been provided, evidently for whoever manned the lookout post to sit on. But Frank noticed that its cover was hinged. Inside was a hand mirror and a pair of binoculars in a case.

Joe eagerly tried out the latter, swinging the glasses in all directions. "Wow! What a view! You can even make out ships offshore!"

As he handed the binoculars to his brother, both boys blinked in a sudden dazzling glare.

"Hey, someone's flashing sunlight at us!" Joe blurted.

"Signaling," Frank exclaimed a moment later as the flashes continued. "Joe, I bet that's what the mirror in the box is for!"

"You're right. But it's not Morse."

"Some private code, probably." As he trained the binoculars on the source of the flashes, Frank found himself focusing on a large gray vehicle parked off the highway some distance to the west. "The signals are coming from a big motor camper," he reported.

"Oh, oh!" Joe muttered uneasily. "If they've got binoculars, too, they can probably see us up here.

In fact, I bet that's why they started signaling!"

"Right! They probably parked there just to keep watch. They must've been expecting someone to show up in this lookout post."

"Let's hope they can't see our faces clearly, or they'll know we're not members of the gang!"

The sun flashes had stopped momentarily, but then resumed faster than ever.

"If they get wise," Frank said, "they may come looking for us. And they might discover Chet in the car!"

"Why don't we take the hand mirror and signal back?" Joe suggested.

"How can we? We don't know their code."

"So what? They'll probably just think we made an accidental goof. While they're trying to figure out our message, we'll have time to get back to the car."

Frank was dubious, but agreed.

Joe promptly snatched up the hand mirror and began beaming sun flashes in the direction of the camper, trying to repeat the pattern he had just seen.

When he paused, the boys waited anxiously, but there were no further signals in response.

"They've clammed up," Frank muttered. "I'm not sure I like that."

Neither did Joe. But before he could say anything, both were startled by sounds from below of someone moving through the underbrush.

"Hear that?" Joe hissed to his brother.

"I'll say I do! Whoever it is, they're coming this way. Let's get out of here."

Fearing they might be trapped, the Hardys hastily clambered down the oak trunk and sought cover among the dense shrubbery and forest brush.

Within moments they could hear at least two persons moving about and beating the undergrowth with sticks.

"They're searching for us!" Joe whispered.

Frank nodded. "They didn't have time to come from the camper, though. These guys must have been on their way here already!"

The boys dared not raise their heads to see what was going on, but voices reached their ears.

"We saw 'em climbing down!" one searcher growled. "They must be around here somewhere!"

"I know. They didn't have time to get away," the other one agreed, and poked his stick deep into the shrubbery.

"Where's the dog?" the first man asked.

"On the boat. Why?"

"Because we're wasting our time. He could rout out those snoopers in seconds. Let's go back and get him—and we'll pick up some gas grenades while we're at it. If the Doberman can't sniff 'em out, we'll see how they like a dose of Mace!"

"That's a good idea, but what if they disappear while we're gone?"

"H'm. Tell you what. You stay here while I get the dog. If they stir somewhere, just follow them. Turn your walkie-talkie on so you can tell me where they are, okay?"

"Right."

The boys heard a set of footsteps retreating, while the other man kept walking around the area with his stick. When he was some distance away, Frank whispered to Joe.

"We can't wait until that other creep comes back with the Doberman!"

"You're right. Should we run for it while this guy's a little bit away from us?"

"No, we've got to jump him, otherwise he'll alert his partner with his walkie-talkie. Wait until he comes closer again. We've got to make sure he doesn't get away!"

Soon the footsteps became louder and the boys could hear the *swish* of the man's stick against the foliage.

"Now!" Frank hissed.

Both boys jumped up and caught the stranger by surprise. Before he had a chance to swing his weapon, Frank barreled into him and swung a fist at the man's jaw. With a grunt, the crook fell backward. Frank threw himself on top of the man and wrested the stick from his hand. At that moment the stranger rolled quickly to the right, throwing Frank off balance. But before the man had a chance to regain his feet, Joe hooked an arm around his neck and pushed him down again.

"I've got a good hold on him," Joe called to his brother. "Find some vines so we can tie him up!"

Frank quickly ripped out stout vines from the ground and bound the man's wrists and ankles. Then he took the scarf the stranger was wearing around his neck and gagged him with it.

"This way he can't alert his buddy over the walkie-talkie," the boy declared. "Come on, Joe, let's get out of here now!"

The brothers bolted away from the area of the tree platform and rushed toward their car.

Suddenly, Joe tripped and fell headlong on the ground.

Frank, who was slightly ahead of his brother, heard Joe's muffled scream and turned back. "Did you hurt yourself?" he asked anxiously.

Joe was about to get up, but fell back in pain. "I twisted my ankle! I don't think I can stand!"

Suddenly, in the distance, both boys heard vicious barking. Visions of the Doberman's angry jaws danced before their eyes. Determinedly, Frank reached for his brother, realizing the barking was becoming louder and louder!

14 A Warning in Red

"Come on, lean on me!" Frank panted and pulled Joe to his feet.

The younger Hardy let out a groan, but stayed up, his arm around Frank's shoulder. With his brother's support, he hobbled toward the car as fast as he could.

When they arrived, Chet Morton stirred from his comfortable, dozing position and opened the door for them. "What's wrong?" he asked.

"Joe's hurt his ankle and the crooks are after us with a Doberman!" Frank said.

"What!"

Just then the boys heard the dog again. He seemed to be getting angrier every second. Frank slid behind the wheel while Chet pulled Joe into the front seat. "Let's get out of here!" the chubby boy yelled. Frank had already started the motor, and with a cloud of exhaust the yellow sports car sped down the road.

"Now tell me what happened," Chet demanded.

Joe related their adventure at the lookout post, rubbing his ankle with both hands.

"Wow!" Chet blurted. "If they'd caught you guys, I might've been next!"

Joe grinned. "Unless that doggie would have picked up your scent on the way and gotten you first!"

Chet made a face. "I shudder just thinking of it. What about that camper? Could you see where it was parked?"

"Yes, we should be coming to it soon," said Frank. "From the treetop, it looked as if it was about half a mile or so beyond that cranberry bog we just passed. It was close to a point where the road makes a sharp turn to the right."

"Here's the turn," Joe muttered.

As Frank swung the wheel, he caught a glimpse of Chet's chubby-cheeked face in the rearview mirror. The stout youth looked tense and apprehensive at the prospect of a possible confrontation with what-ever trigger-happy crooks might be lurking in the camper. But he had the heart and build of a bear, and Frank knew he could be counted on in any tight spot.

As it turned out, however, the big, gray camper van was nowhere in sight!

"Hey, what's that red stuff on the road?" Joe exclaimed.

Blood was the thought that immediately came to all three boys' minds. But as Frank stepped on the brake and slowed for a closer look, they saw that big red letters had been painted on the blacktop surface of the highway:

HARDYS—YOU'LL GET YOURS!

Just above the warning was a crude skull and crossbones!

Chet gulped. "Looks as if you found the right place!"

"And it also looks as if whoever was here had good binoculars to recognize our faces," Joe remarked grimly.

"No doubt we're up against El Diablo's gang," Frank added.

Just then a buzz sounded from the dashboard radio, and a red light blinked, indicating an incoming call. Joe answered and heard Sam Radley's voice over the speaker.

"What's up, Sam?"

"I finally got a 'make' on that guy you called

about. If I'm right, his name's Francis Jerome Waulker"—the private operative spelled out the last name—"better known as 'Whitey' Waulker. There's a fugitive warrant out on him. He's wanted for a long list of crimes, including car theft, armed robbery, and felonious assault."

"Jupiter! Sounds like he could be real bad news," said Joe, thinking of Waulker's attack on his brother.

"You better believe it! What's more, he's a three-time loser. If he gets convicted one more time, he could get sent up for life. So don't expect him to surrender meekly to the law, if you run into him again."

"Thanks for warning us, Sam."

"Just don't take any chances, that's all. But say, here's a bit more pleasant news, if you're interested," the detective went on. "Do I understand you fellows are looking for that old-time pirate's treasure while you're in the Pine Barrens, the one that got written up in the newspaper?"

"Trying to, anyhow," Joe responded with a dry chuckle, "though I can't say we're making much progress. Why? Got any hot leads for us?"

"Well, I don't know how hot it is, but this might be of some help. There's a local historical society in a coastal town called Tuckerton that keeps tabs on all sorts of folklore and historical records relating to the Pine Barrens. The secretary of the society helped me out on a case a couple of years ago. You might try him for information."

"Sounds like a great idea!" Joe said enthusiastically, and took down the man's name and address.

"Wait a minute before you sign off," Frank exclaimed suddenly. Taking the microphone from his brother, he asked, "Sam, would you ever have heard of a lawyer named Verrill—Ambrose Verrill?"

The boys were surprised at the short, harsh laugh over the radio loudspeaker. "I'll say I have. What do you want to know about him?"

"Anything *you* know."

"Well, I've run into him half a dozen times at the county courthouse when I've gone there to testify at trials. Verrill's more of a shady ambulance chaser than a reputable attorney. Matter of fact, he is under investigation by the State Bar Association."

"How come?"

"One of his clients accused him of absconding with a valuable old document, which he was supposed to have put in a safe-deposit box. Verrill claims it was misplaced by accident, but the Bar Association doesn't buy his excuse."

Frank whistled, then told Sam about their investigation. "No doubt that valuable old document was Jem Taggart's letter," he concluded.

"I'm sure it was," Sam agreed.

After Frank had replaced the microphone, he

turned to Joe. "No wonder Verrill got so upset when he heard we had a photostat of the letter. Whoever made that copy might be able to prove the letter was in Verrill's possession!"

"Which could land Verrill in jail if he swiped it from one of his clients," Joe said.

Finally the trio arrived back at camp. The pain in Joe's ankle had subsided quite a bit and he was able to limp around.

Frank proposed an early supper, since he had a theory that he wanted to check out that very evening.

Over charcoal-broiled steaks and fries, he told the others, "I've got a hunch that one of the Diablo gang's rackets may be helping wanted crooks to get out of the country."

Joe grinned. "Something tells me our minds are working in the same groove."

"Kerric was one of the gang's customers, right?"

The younger Hardy boy nodded in agreement. "And now Whitey Waulker's another."

"What do you mean 'one of their customers'?" Biff Hooper broke in.

"Kerric probably paid the gang plenty to smuggle him out of the United States before the FBI could nab him," Frank explained. "But a state trooper spotted and arrested him just as his disappearing act was about to get started."

"How was it supposed to work?"

Frank took the little plastic devil doll out of his pocket as he replied, "Let's say every customer gets one of these Jersey Devil figures when he first shells out money to the gang. They tell him to go to the Pirate's Tavern on the edge of the Pine Barrens and use the doll for identification."

"Another gang member meets him at the tavern," Joe conjectured, "and gives him an ultraviolet lamp and a map showing how to get to the trail through the woods."

"Right." Frank nodded. "So he waits till it gets dark and then uses the lamp to follow the fluorescent blaze marks on the trees, which eventually lead him to the big, spooky Jersey Devil figure, marking the gang's lookout post."

"What happens then?" Tony Prito asked.

"There's a river or creek close by that must run clear to the coast," Joe said. "We glimpsed stretches of it from the tree platform, and we also heard those guys who were searching for us today talk about going back to the boat."

"Exactly," Frank said. "So when the crook gets to the lookout post, one of the gang meets him there and takes him downriver by boat. From there he's whisked out to sea and aboard a ship headed for some foreign port."

"Pretty neat!" Chet exclaimed.

"That's not all," Frank went on. "We saw Whitey Waulker with a lamp at the Pirate's Tavern today. He probably had a map, too. If our theory's correct, he may show up tonight at the turnoff to the secret trail."

Tony grinned. "And you figure if he does, we can nail him!"

Not wanting to leave the camp deserted, it was decided that Joe and Tony should remain behind. Joe's ankle still hurt him somewhat, but he was hoping that if he stayed off it as much as possible, he would be all right in the morning.

Dusk had fallen by the time Frank, Biff, and Chet reached the turnoff point to the trail through the woods. Chet, who was at the wheel, drove deep in among the trees on the opposite side of the road, so that the car would be out of sight to anyone approaching along the highway from either direction. Then the three boys got out and made their way through the underbrush to a point where they could keep watch and go into action quickly.

"What happens when he shows up?" Biff asked.

"We'll give him a chance to turn off onto the trail," Frank replied. "Then we follow him on foot and grab him as soon as he gets out of his car."

"I have an idea," Chet said, surveying a tree next to him. "I'll climb up to get a better view of the road. This way I can warn you when I see him!"

Before Frank could object, Chet had already pulled himself into the bottom branches of the tree.

"Don't go too high," Frank warned. "It'll take you too long to come down!"

"I won't," Chet replied. "I figured just about ten feet—"

Crunch! There was the noise of a breaking limb, and the next moment Chet hit the ground with a thud and an involuntary cry.

"*Shh!*" Frank urged, worried that they would be heard. "You can't be hurt. You didn't fall very far, so stop advertising that we're here!"

"Sorry," Chet mumbled.

Biff couldn't help but chuckle. "And here we were worried that you wouldn't come down fast enough!"

"Go ahead, laugh," Chet grumbled. "I was only trying to help!"

Suddenly, Frank held up a hand. They heard the sound of a car in the distance.

"That may be Waulker!" Chet hissed.

Sure enough, the vehicle came closer and slowed almost to a halt at the turnoff. But as it was about to pull onto the dirt trail, a brilliant spotlight suddenly blazed out of the darkness. At the same time, a loud voice shouted, "Keep going!"

15 The Spooky Glow

An instant later, a loud volley of warning shots pierced the air! Instead of turning, the car speeded up and continued along the highway!

For a moment, the boys were dumbfounded. Then Frank said angrily, "The crooks must have heard us, so they told the guy to scram. Let's go after him!"

The three ran to their car and piled in, afraid to be shot at any moment. But nothing happened as Frank slid behind the wheel, gunned the engine, and swiftly maneuvered out from among the trees.

"I guess they didn't see us," Chet murmured. "But they know we're around! Did anyone get a good look at the driver?"

Biff shook his head. "Not me."

"Neither did I," said Frank, "but it had to be Waulker. Who else would be turning onto that trail after dark?"

The getaway car, a dark-colored Chevy, was barely visible far ahead. The engine of the Hardys' yellow sports sedan, however, was tuned for maximum power and acceleration, and by skillful driving Frank steadily narrowed the distance between them.

"What if this guy's armed?" Biff muttered.

"Don't worry, we won't do anything stupid, or try any dumb heroics," Frank assured him. "Sam Radley warned that Waulker could be dangerous. I just want to trail him to wherever he's going and maybe help the police round him up."

Even at closer range, it was difficult to make out the exact color or model of the car. And the sudden glare of the spotlight back at the trail turnoff had momentarily blinded the boys, preventing them from identifying either the driver or his vehicle. Nevertheless, Frank switched on their dashboard radio to call the Red Lion barracks of the State Police west of the pine woods, hoping that roadblocks might be set up to trap the fugitive.

Just then, he saw something hurtle backward from the driver's window of the getaway car. A sound of breaking glass was heard and jagged bottle fragments glittered in their headlight glare. Frank swerved desperately, but at high speed it was impossible to avoid the scattered road hazard just ahead.

Blam! There was a momentary report as one of the front tires punctured, and the yellow sports sedan went into a terrifying spin!

Both Hardy boys had been well taught by their father how to react in a driving crisis. Frank steered and braked in such a way as to bring the car to the quickest, smoothest halt possible. Even so, it wound up broadside across the road, with its rear end only inches from the trees bordering the shoulder.

"Nice going, pal!" Biff congratulated Frank after all three boys had collected themselves.

Frank shrugged bitterly. "There go our chances of nabbing Waulker!"

They got out to inspect the damage. Luckily, only the left front tire had gone flat, but twenty minutes would be lost by the time they put on the spare. Not knowing what evasive route Waulker might have taken, much less his car's precise description or license number, the boys realized there was little use in contacting the police.

"We do know one thing, though," Frank reflected when they finally headed back to camp.

"What's that?" Biff queried.

"If Diablo's gang was going to smuggle Waulker out of the country tonight, they'd expect whatever ship they planned on using to be there."

"Hey, good thinking!" Chet said. "If you're right, the ship may heave to somewhere close offshore during the next twenty-four hours and wait for their signal."

"Right. And if we tell my father," Frank went on, "maybe he can alert the Coast Guard to keep watch for it, or take other steps to get the goods on Diablo."

"Call him right now, Frank!" Biff advised.

The Hardy boy transmitted the secret code signal which he and his brother used to contact their father in emergencies. But there was no reply. As they approached a crossroads gas station, which was closed for the night, Frank saw a telephone booth outside and pulled up beside it.

"I have an idea" he announced. "I'll call Jack Wayne. If we can't reach Dad, maybe we can get Jack to fly us offshore so we can try spotting the ship ourselves."

"Good idea!" Chet said. Jack Wayne was a charter pilot in Bayport who often flew Fenton Hardy and his two sons on special assignments.

Frank hopped out, plugged the pay phone with coins, and placed a call to Jack Wayne's company, the Ace Air Service, at the Bayport airfield. Presently, he returned to the car, shaking his head. "No luck. The girl in the office says Jack's in Dayton and won't be back till tomorrow."

"At least we've tried," said Biff. "If Waulker doesn't escape tonight, the gang probably won't try to smuggle him out to the ship during the daylight hours. Maybe there'll still be time to look for him tomorrow."

Arriving back at camp, the trio told their two friends everything that had happened. Joe and Tony, who had no news of their own to report, listened eagerly to the exciting account of the evening's events.

"Wow! Sounds like you guys had all the fun!" cracked Tony.

"If that's the right word for it," Frank said wryly.

The boys soon turned in as the nightly silence settled over the camp, broken only by the drowsy chirp of crickets and the occasional explosive boom of a diving nighthawk. But presently other, more mysterious noises made them poke their heads out of their tents.

"Did you guys hear that?" Chet hissed.

"We sure did," Joe replied. "Sounded like a low foghorn."

"Jumpin' catfish! Look at that!" Biff gasped, pointing as he spoke.

A weird greenish light could be seen glowing

144

among the trees near the foot of the hillside!

This time the boys had no intention of being decoyed away from the real scene of action. After a hasty conversation it was decided that Biff and Chet would remain behind to guard the camp, while the others would investigate the weird glow. Joe's ankle barely hurt any more, and he was eager to join his brother and Tony.

Cautiously the trio made their way down the slope, each clutching a stout stick with which to defend himself from possible attack.

As they approached the source of the illumination, the light suddenly went out—but not before Frank saw something that made his blood boil.

"Look out!" he shouted to his companions. "It's a trap!"

At the same moment, Joe tripped on a trailing vine, lost his footing, and stumbled forward!

16 Gallows Clue

There was no way Joe could stop himself from falling. Tony, too, had heard Frank's warning cry. He thrust out his hand in time to grab Joe's arm and jerk him out of the danger zone.

Joe landed on one knee, gasping. The yellow glow of Frank's flashlight revealed what he had almost stumbled into—*a steel-jawed bear trap!*

Joe swallowed hard. "That thing could break a guy's leg!" he whispered.

"And don't think those teeth wouldn't gouge into your flesh and muscle!" Frank added grimly.

At that moment, a sneering laugh rang out in the darkness. The sound brought the three boys instantly to attention, and Joe sprang to his feet.

"It came from over there!" Tony pointed.

As he spoke, they saw a figure break from cover and dart through the darkness. Frank swung his flashlight and pinned the fugitive in its glare.

"It's Verrill!" he cried.

The three youths angrily took after the man. With his long legs, Verrill might well have gotten away, but the boys' pursuit of him was fueled with burning rage. A mere dirty trick to lure them away from camp was one thing, but a deliberate attempt to cause them serious bodily harm was another. They were determined to catch the lawyer, even if it meant running both him and themselves to the point of exhaustion.

Verrill plunged through dense thickets and zigzagged back and forth among the trees, trying desperately to shake them off, but the Hardys and Tony closed in relentlessly. Never for more than a few moments at a time could he evade the probing beam of Frank's flashlight.

Soon Verrill was far more winded than the boys. His chest was heaving and his legs were rubbery when Frank lunged through the air and finally brought him down with a flying tackle.

"Let go of me!" Verrill blustered as Joe and Tony joined in his capture, each of them pinning one of his arms.

"Do you realize what might've happened if one of

us had walked into that bear trap?" Frank gritted. "My brother nearly did!"

"I ought to punch you right in the nose for that!" Joe added.

The lawyer looked sullenly from one boy to another as they jerked him roughly to his feet. "I don't know what you're talking about," he muttered.

"Oh, no?" Frank's eyes drilled into him coldly. Then maybe you'd rather have us get the State Police so you can explain to them. If I remember correctly from what Dad told us about criminal law, there's a felony charge called 'reckless endangerment,' and the penalty if convicted can be pretty severe."

"Don't try to bluff me, Sonny!" Verrill's voice took on a deep, courtroom boom as he sought to impress his captors. "False arrest is also a serious charge, and that's what you'd be facing if you try any such nonsense. I'll remind you you're talking to an experienced *attorney*!"

Much to his astonishment, the Hardys laughed in his face.

"Tell us about it!" Joe said. "We've had you checked out, Mr. Verrill. You're in serious trouble with the Bar Association!"

Verrill's bluster suddenly evaporated. His open-mouthed dismay showed how completely the Hardys had demolished his false front.

Frank followed up fast. He had noticed that in addition to his flannel shirt and khaki pants, Verrill was wearing athletic shoes with heavy rubber soles of the kind that always have a distinctive pattern of cleats.

"No wonder you were so careful to brush away your footprints the other day when you raided our camp and stole our food," he remarked. "But we got enough fingerprints off the van to prove our case— if we need to, that is. You were probably heading for your car when we nabbed you just now, so it must be parked somewhere near here. It wouldn't surprise me if we found some of our stuff still stashed in it."

Again Verrill's expression showed that Frank's guess had hit home. The final blow came when Tony suddenly exclaimed, "Hey, look!" and pounced on a pale, oblong object lying among the trampled grass and brush.

"That's mine!" Verrill cried and tried to snatch it away from Tony, only to have his arms quickly pinioned again by the Hardys. "It fell out of my pocket when you fellows struggled with me!" the man whined. "Give it back to me!"

"Well, well, well," said Frank as he looked at the

149

transparent plastic envelope containing a weather-beaten, yellowed old document. He removed it and unfolded it in the glow of the flashlight.

Frank whistled, and Joe whooped triumphantly. "That's the original letter from Jem Taggart to his gang!"

"Which you stole from a client," Frank said accusingly to Ambrose Verrill. "This is clear evidence that you committed a crime!"

Verrill's face seemed to crumple, almost as if he were on the verge of tears. His hands jittered and his manner became cringing. "Look, boys, do we have to make such a big thing out of this? The fact is that the letter got misplaced. It just turned up this morning among a bunch of other papers in my briefcase. I was going to return it to my client as soon as I got back to Bayport. I'll admit it was, well, pretty high-handed of me, raiding your camp and all, but you must remember, I've been under terrible emotional strain! As for this prank to-night—"

"Some prank!" Joe cut in sarcastically.

"It was ill-judged, I see that now," the lawyer said. "Had one of you been hurt, no one would have been more upset than I. Put it down to the pressure I've been under."

Verrill paused to pull a flashlight out of his pocket, to show the boys how he had wrapped green cellophane over the lens to produce the greenish glow. "You see, it was just meant as a joke—a harmless joke—though in poor taste, I'll admit. As for Jem Taggart's treasure, you fellows feel free to go right on looking for it! I see no reason for any conflict between us at all. Perhaps we might even join forces and search for it together. I'm sure my client would agree. Then, if we find it, we can all split the fortune. What would you say to that?"

"Nuts," Frank responded bluntly. Verrill's face fell as the elder Hardy boy went on. "For the time being we'll hang onto Jem Taggart's letter until we can turn it over to the police as criminal evidence. It'll be up to your client to decide whether or not he wants you prosecuted for theft."

Verrill slunk off dejectedly and the boys returned to their camp. Early next morning, the Hardys drove into the pleasant seaside town of Tuckerton to consult the local historical society. The address Sam Radley had given them turned out to be a fine, beautiful house, more than a hundred years old, now occupied by a retired businessman named Soames who acted as secretary of the society.

He greeted the boys with a pleased twinkle in his eyes as they shook hands. "Matter of fact, I've been wondering if you fellows might come around. I read that newspaper item telling how you were interested in looking for that load of silver plate supposedly buried by the Outlaw of the Pine Barrens."

"Do you think it really exists, Mr. Soames?" Joe asked.

"Well, I can only say there's no reason to believe it's ever been found."

Frank said, "Do you have any information relating to Jem Taggart?"

"Oh, yes, indeed!" The elderly secretary nodded. "We have a whole file drawer full of material, such as photostats of old courthouse records and so on, which you're welcome to look at."

He led the boys into a large adjoining room filled with bookcases, file cabinets, and glass display cases containing historical relics.

Frank and Joe were excited when they saw the contents of the file drawer. Mr. Soames helpfully pointed out the most pertinent documents, then left the boys alone to glean through the material.

They learned that Jem Taggart himself had been captured near Tuckerton on March 4, 1781. "The day after he wrote that letter!" Joe exclaimed.

His two cronies, Xavier and Whaleboat Charlie, were nabbed on March 5th and 6th at different places near the coast.

"Which means they must have gotten caught when they tried to join Jem for the purpose of splitting the treasure," said Frank.

"And apparently they didn't have any of the silver on them," Joe added.

All three were tried and condemned for various serious crimes. According to an old newspaper account, just before mounting the gallows, Jem uttered a mocking laugh and chuckled to the attending parson, "You'll find another dead man ten paces north—if you're lucky!"

Joe frowned as he read the old newspaper story for a second time. "Those words 'ten paces north' tie in with the letter, which says 'ten paces north as crow flies.' But what exactly does that mean?"

Frank shrugged. "Search me. But I bet the letter X that Chet spotted on the lean-to stands for that one member of the gang named Xavier!"

"If we only could find out what 'fishhook' means," Joe said.

Mr. Soames could offer no clues either, but promised to get in touch with the boys if he thought of anything. The Hardys thanked him and headed back to camp.

On the way, they stopped at Bosley's cabin.

"You two back again?" the man grumbled.

"We're hoping you passed on what we told you," Frank said, "about Rupert Price being cleared of that murder charge and inheriting a lot of money."

"I've told you, Rupert died of pneumonia!"

Joe threw his brother an exasperated glance and

shrugged. As they turned away, Della ran up. "Do you have to go so soon?" she asked, disappointed.

"I think your daddy wants it that way, honey," Frank said. Then he noticed her hugging her hand-carved wooden doll, and suddenly remembered that Rupert Price had enjoyed whittling and wood-carving.

"My, that's a pretty doll you have," he told Della. "Where did you get it?"

"Go on inside, Della," Bosley said sharply. "These boys have to be getting on."

His daughter obeyed reluctantly, and the Hardys got back into their car and drove off.

"That just about clinches it," Joe said. "Bosley knew why you were asking Della, so he—"

A buzz sounded from the dashboard and he switched on the radio. A familiar voice crackled over the loudspeaker. "*G calling H-1 and H-2. Do you read me?*"

17 *The Silver Fishhook*

"H-2 here," Joe replied. "We read you, Aunt Gertrude. Come in, please."

Aunt Gertrude's tone was sharp as mustard. "Are you all right? And where's H-1?"

"Sitting right beside me. Why, what's up?"

"We just had a phone call from Jack Wayne. He says Frank tried to get hold of him last night. Your mother and I were worried one of you boys might've strayed off and gotten lost in the wilderness, so you needed a plane to help look for him from the air."

Joe chuckled. "No, it was nothing like that, Aunt Gertrude. We think there's a smuggling operation going on down here that ties in with Dad's case.

Frank wanted Jack to see if he could spot the smugglers' ship offshore."

"Hmph! Sounds dangerous to me. You boys better be careful, understand?"

"Yes, ma'am. Over and out." Joe signed off with a grin. Despite Aunt Gertrude's constant fretting over her nephews' safety, he knew she was secretly proud of their work.

Frank detoured to the nearest gas station to return Jack Wayne's call. Jack himself answered, and the young detective explained the situation.

"Is there any place around here where you could pick us up?" Frank ended.

"Sure, there's a small airfield the fire wardens use right there in the Pine Barrens."

Jack Wayne described its location. By consulting their map, Frank saw that the field was only about a twenty-minute drive from their camp at Cedar Knob. A time was fixed later that afternoon when the plane would land and then take off with the brothers for a survey flight just offshore from the coastal edge of the Barrens.

As Frank hung up and left the phone booth, Joe was paying the service station attendant who had filled the tank of their yellow sports sedan.

"By the way," Frank said casually, "my girlfriend collects dolls. I'd like to bring her one from the Pine

Barrens as a souvenir. We've heard there's a skilled woodcarver down here. Would you by any chance know who he is, or where we could find him?"

"Oh, sure," said the attendant, "you mean Rube Peters. He's always whittling dolls for little kids."

The attendant gave the Hardy boys exact directions for finding the woodcarver's cabin. They thanked him and drove off.

"Nice going," Joe congratulated his brother. "That's got to be more than just coincidence—him having the same initials as the guy we're looking for. 'Rube Peters' must be the alias Rupert Price has been going under."

"Sure sounds that way," Frank agreed hopefully. "But let's wait and see."

After lunching with their pals at the camp, the Hardys drove to the cabin that the gas station attendant had described to them. It was set well back from the dirt road they were following, behind a pleasant screen of dogwoods and berry bushes. Small and with a veranda in front, it was covered with cedar shakes and looked somewhat neater than most of the weather-beaten houses and tar-paper shacks that the boys had seen deep in the forest.

But their hearts sank when a fat, scowling man came to the door in answer to Joe's knock. He looked nothing whatever like the snapshot Ogden

Price had shown them of his cousin in navy uniform.

"Mr. Peters?" Frank said lamely.

"Who wants to know?" the fat man growled.

"We do," Joe spoke up. "We heard you were quite a woodcarver, so we came to see your work. We'd like to buy something if any of it is for sale."

"I've nothing to sell," was the gruff reply. Then the door slammed in their faces.

The Hardys looked at each other, then reluctantly turned away from the house.

"He sure didn't look like that picture of Rupert Price!" Joe muttered under his breath.

"No, and I don't think he *is* Rupert Price—or even Rube Peters!" Frank replied in a low voice.

"How come?"

"Willard Bosley may have warned Rupert that we're still looking for him—maybe even that we spotted a wooden doll he'd carved. Rupert might have arranged for someone to take his place, if any strangers came looking for the local woodcarver."

"Something tells me you could be right," Joe murmured glumly. "But if he's hiding inside, and using that fat guy to front for him, how do we flush him out?"

Instead of replying, Frank suddenly appeared to catch his foot among some matted weeds. He lost his balance and fell headlong!

"Hey, are you all right?" Joe exclaimed as his

brother gave a loud groan and rubbed his hand gingerly over one leg.

Frank struggled to get up, only to utter another cry of pain, then flopped back on the ground. "I—I think my leg may be broken!"

"Don't try to stand on it! Just stay there until I get help!" Joe instructed him and hastily turned back to the house.

The fat man was scowling at them from the window. He had the door open even before Joe had time to knock. "What's the matter?" he demanded gruffly.

"My brother fell and thinks he's broken his leg," Joe said. "Can you give me a hand?"

The fat man stood glaring in the doorway with his mouth open, obviously uncertain of what to say. As he hesitated, Joe heard another voice from inside the cabin. "Maybe I can help, Gabe."

"But—" Gabe began to object.

"It's okay. I'll handle this."

A lean, muscular, dark-haired man now emerged into view, as if he had been standing somewhere just inside the doorway. He patted the fat man, who was evidently named Gabe, on the shoulder and came out of the cabin.

"Let's take a look at your brother's leg," he said calmly.

Frank, who was still lying on the ground, watched

as the two walked down the footpath toward him. "Mr. Price?" he inquired.

The dark-haired man stopped short with a frown. "Don't tell me your broken leg was just a trick?"

"I'm afraid so, sir," Frank confessed, standing up easily. "I understand you were a navy medical corpsman and planned to become a doctor. I had a hunch you wouldn't feel right about letting an injured person go without first aid, just so you could stay in hiding."

There was a moment of exasperated silence. The Hardys wondered if Rupert Price might give way to an angry outburst. Instead, his expression gradually relaxed into a wry smile. "Well, it looks as though you guessed right, Son," he conceded. "I suppose you two are those young detectives, the Hardy boys?"

"Yes, sir. I'm Frank and this is my brother Joe."

They shook hands, and Price explained, "There isn't much available in the way of medical care down here in the Pine Barrens, so I've tried to help out whenever I could. Actually, I've learned a lot from the old-timers around here—I mean, about Indian medicines and herb remedies you can make from plants growing wild in the woods. Anyhow, the people in these parts are loyal friends, and they're grateful for whatever little doctoring I've done, so they've tried to cover up for me, even though they know I'm wanted by the law. I hope you won't hold that against them."

"Don't worry about that, Mr. Price," Frank assured him. "There's nothing to hold against them because you're no longer wanted by the law. That's what my brother and I tried to tell your friend, Mr. Bosley, but he wouldn't believe us."

Rupert Price nodded. "He told me. But I'm not sure *I* believe it."

"It's what your cousin, Ogden Price, claims. He said you both have an uncle, who recently died and left an estate worth over a million dollars—most of which will go to you. He's only supposed to get about two hundred and fifty thousand dollars of that, but he'll inherit the whole estate if you don't show up to claim your share."

Frank went on to explain that Ogden now felt remorseful for not having helped Rupert prove his innocence years before when he was wrongfully accused. So now he was trying to ease his conscience by finding his cousin and making sure he received his full inheritance.

Rupert Price looked somewhat dazed on hearing all this, but his expression soon settled into a worried frown. "H'm, you've certainly given me food for thought," he said. "But I'm still not certain I trust Ogden. We never did get along. For all I know, this could be a trick on his part to make me give myself up, and then maybe forfeit my inheritance by being sent to prison for a crime I never committed."

"I doubt that very much," Frank said. "Anyhow, we're not going to send the police after you. We did take Ogden's story at face value, but we'll check it out, and if it turns out your cousin has lied to us, we'll do everything we can to help clear your name."

"Thanks for that, boys." Rupert Price smiled and gave both of the Hardys a warm handshake.

Before leaving, they told him about their hunt for Jem Taggart's secret treasure and asked if the word clue, 'fishhook,' meant anything to him.

Rupert thought for a moment. "I've a feeling I've heard that name before, from some of the old-time Piney woodsmen," he said. "My guess would be that it's a place name—maybe for one of the old ghost towns in the Pine Barrens. But that's about all I can tell you."

Frank and Joe drove to the fire wardens' airfield. A short time later, the pilot, Jack Wayne, landed there in his sleek, twin-engine plane, *Skyhappy Sal*, and the Hardys took off with him to scout for any sign of the ship Diablo's gang was expecting.

The plane winged coastward, giving the boys a magnificent view of the vast pine forest. Far ahead they could make out the blue-green expanse of the ocean, dotted with fishing boats.

Suddenly, Joe grabbed his brother's shoulder and pointed downward. "Look!" he exclaimed.

Below, among the trees, could be seen the silver outline of a creek or river. *It was curved in the shape of a fishhook!*

18 Ten Paces North

Frank gasped with excitement as he saw how the stream curved through the wooded terrain. "That could be the 'fishhook' Jem Taggart meant in his letter to the rest of the gang!"

"I'll bet anything it is!" Joe declared. "And that means we must be somewhere over the treasure right now!"

"Any place you could land around here, Jack?" Frank asked.

The pilot scanned the scene below them, then shook his head. "No way. I don't see any spot within miles that's bare enough or smooth enough to use for a landing strip."

"Then we'll have to jump!" Frank decided.

Jack Wayne flashed the boys a worried glance. "Sure you know what you're doing?"

"It's the quickest, simplest way," Joe argued. "We could waste hours trying to find the fishhook if we had to hike in from the nearest road!"

"What about your dad—would he approve?"

"I'm sure he would," Frank told the pilot. "He taught us skydiving himself."

"I suggest you go back to the airfield and get our car," Joe said. "Would you mind driving to the road point nearest to the stream, so we can join you later?"

Jack grinned. "Will do. And I expect you to find the treasure, hear?"

Skyhappy Sal carried parachuting gear as part of her regular equipment. The Hardys zipped themselves into coveralls, strapped on backpack chutes, then donned goggles, helmets, and gloves. Their high-laced hiking boots would serve for the jump.

Jack Wayne banked and circled to the right, maneuvering the plane into position, then headed into the wind directly over the fishhook-shaped stream. One by one, in quick succession, Frank and Joe poised in the open doorway and launched themselves into the air.

Both dropped in "stable-fall" position—face down, body arched, arms and legs spread out and slightly bent. Moments later, as each pulled his

ripcord handle, the parachute popped out, opening the canopy with a jolt. Presently, the two boys felt the exhilarating thrill of floating down through wind-swept space toward the earth below.

By "slipping" their chutes expertly, the Hardys steered themselves toward their target. They landed close together on the same bank of the stream, touching down feet first. They whirled fast as they fell forward so as to take the main shock in a sitting position, with a quick hand tug on the risers to help cushion the blow.

Scrambling to their feet, the boys unsnapped their canopies and pulled off helmet and goggles to exchange satisfied grins.

"Not bad, I must say!" Joe declared.

"I think Dad would have approved our form," Frank agreed, smiling.

They waved at *Skyhappy Sal*, watching Jack Wayne circle and dip the wings, then head toward the airfield. Then they stripped off their gloves, harness, and coveralls and rolled up their chutes with practiced skill before turning their attention to the problem of the treasure.

"You know, I was thinking on the way down," Frank remarked, "trying to put the whole picture together, and I've got a hunch about the way things happened."

"Great! Let's hear it," Joe said eagerly.

"Well, first of all, that carving Chet discovered on the lean-to . . . 'Fishhook X' . . ."

"You figured the X stands for Xavier," Joe broke in.

"Right. Let's say that's his signature. But why did he carve the word 'Fishhook'?"

"As a message?"

"Right." Frank nodded. "That's my guess too. Maybe Whaleboat Charlie, the other member of the gang, wasn't with him at camp when the Indian runner brought the letter from Jem Taggart. It's not likely Xavier would be carrying any paper or ink with him, so he just carved the word 'fishhook' to let Charlie know where they were to meet the gang leader and divide the treasure."

"And when Charlie got back, he saw the message and followed Xavier," Joe chimed in eagerly. "But they all got caught before they could dig up the treasure."

"We hope!" Frank concluded with a wry grin.

As the boys surveyed the area where they had landed, they saw that the point of the fishhook was located at an opening in a rocky outcrop where the stream emerged from some underground source, probably draining from higher ground.

"Let's count off ten paces north, like the letter says, and see where it takes us," Joe proposed.

Starting from the point of the hook, they measured the distance. From their aerial inspection of the terrain, they already had a fairly precise bearing, but they used Joe's pocket compass to check and make sure their steps were heading north.

This maneuver brought them in among the trees fringing the bank of the stream, and it was immediately apparent that they had correctly followed the directions of the Outlaw of the Pine Barrens.

Just ahead lay a rectangular plot of slightly sunken ground. It was topped by small rocks, probably plucked from the streambed. Staring at the rock configuration for a few moments, the boys suddenly realized that if a few of the rocks shifted position slightly, they would form the letters *BJ*!

"Black Jack!" Joe exclaimed. "The guy that Jem said in the letter '*was took bad and died*'!"

Frank nodded again dryly. "What took him bad was probably a cutlass blow from Jem Taggart, or a bang over the head with a rock."

"One person less to share the treasure with," Joe conjectured. "Or maybe Jem suspected Black Jack was planning to double-cross him."

"Whatever the reason was, it looks as if Jem planted him here for keeps." Frank paused and rubbed his jaw thoughtfully before adding, "And the letter says the silver plate was buried under him."

Joe looked at his brother uncertainly. "So what do

we do—get some sticks and start digging?"

"Pretty slow way to tackle the job. We actually need shovels," Frank said. "Do you really want to dig up Black Jack's grave?"

"Not much." Joe's face showed a total lack of enthusiasm, even at the prospect of eventually finding a load of silver plate under the remains of the old-time outlaw.

"Neither do I," Frank admitted. "Besides, now that we've found where Jem buried Black Jack, I'm not so sure I trust Taggart's letter."

Joe frowned, puzzled. "What do you mean?"

"Well, we know Taggart was a real scoundrel. He even killed one member of his own gang. Why trust the other two? If he told them where the treasure was buried, he'd be taking a risk they might get here first and do him out of his share."

"You may have a point there. On the other hand, maybe Black Jack really became ill and died, and Jem buried him."

Frank shrugged. "I doubt it. From all we've read about Taggart, it sounds more like him to pull some dirty trick and try to either get rid of or mislead his own pals."

"It sure does," Joe agreed thoughtfully. "Come to think of it, that could be why that line in the letter—'ten paces north as crow flies'—sounds so funny."

"Not only funny, but downright phony," said Frank. "Maybe a deliberate attempt to mislead Xavier and Charlie. I mean, if the distance is as short as ten paces, why say *as the crow flies*?"

Joe frowned and puckered his brows. "Search me. What's your guess?"

"Yeah, let's hear it, smart boy!" a harsh voice suddenly called out.

The Hardys whirled to see who had spoken. Four men had just stepped out into view from among some trees. The boys' hearts sank as they recognized two of them—the flat-nosed thug whom they had first encountered at the ice-cream parlor in Bayport, and his redhead accomplice!

The third man, much to their surprise, was the curly haired reporter, Nate Grimes, who had come to the Hardys' home on Elm Street to interview them about the treasure of the Outlaw of the Pine Barrens.

But it was the speaker on whom their gaze finally settled—a tall, dark, hook-nosed man. Both Frank and Joe sensed that here was the mastermind whom their father was hunting!

19 Smugglers' Hideout

"El Diablo!" Joe gasped.

The dark-haired, hook-nosed man threw back his head and laughed, displaying brilliant white teeth that seemed even brighter by contrast with his deeply tanned, olive-complected face.

"Smart boy!" he exclaimed in a voice that bore a faint trace of foreign accent. "Seems like Fenton Hardy's two brats take after their old man when it comes to brains—eh, *amigos*?"

His three companions grinned and agreed sarcastically with their leader.

"It almost looks as though you were expecting us," Frank said levelly, fishing for information.

"You might put it that way, kid." Diablo smiled and fingered a pair of high-powered binoculars that hung from a strap around his muscular neck. "Grimes here spotted you two as the Hardy boys when we first saw you floating down from the sky. He recognized you through these glasses, even with your helmets and goggles on."

Nate Grimes blushed slightly as the boys' glances flicked toward him.

"Some newspaper reporter!" Joe muttered scornfully.

"No cracks out of you, kid, if you want to stay healthy!" Grimes shot back. "And don't blame me just 'cause you and your wise-apple brother got suckered so easily!"

"How?" Frank needled. "You mean the way we took you at face value and assumed you really *were* a newspaperman?"

"I'm a reporter, all right—don't worry about that," the curly-haired man retorted. "I'm talking about the way you two swallowed the bait when I sent you that copy of Jem Taggart's letter!"

Diablo's gang, the Hardys now learned, had become suspicious of Ambrose Verrill when he first showed up in the Pine Barrens, fearing he might be a detective or lawman working in cooperation with Fenton Hardy. So they had searched his camp secretly and found the original Taggart letter.

173

Diablo, however, was not convinced that the letter was authentic. He thought the document might be a fake, which Verrill was merely using as a cover to explain his snooping about the woods.

The crooked journalist, Grimes, had come up with the bright idea of photographing the letter and sending a copy to the Hardy boys—and then interviewing them to get their reaction.

This would give him a chance to find out if they took it seriously as a possible clue to Taggart's long-lost treasure. If so, Diablo's gang would know that Verrill was probably not working with Fenton Hardy.

In the event the Hardy boys actually came to the Pine Barrens to search for the silver hoard, so much the better from Diablo's point of view. This would give the gang a chance to keep an eye on them— perhaps even to nab Fenton Hardy himself if he came to visit his sons' camp.

"And if you happened to *find* the treasure," Grimes ended with a nasty smile, "who could ask for anything more?"

"Looks like they found it, all right!" Diablo chuckled, flashing his white teeth again. He had closed in on the boys to see what they were examining when the gang surprised them, and now he pointed triumphantly at the stones loosely forming the letters *BJ*. "Black Jack's grave!"

The other three crooks pressed forward eagerly to see for themselves.

"Hey!" Grimes exclaimed, his eyes lighting up greedily. "If Taggart's letter means anything, the treasure's down there, right underneath Black Jack's bones!"

Diablo turned and barked out orders to Flat Nose and the red-haired thug. "Go get some spades from the camper!"

Frank and Joe glanced at each other, both realizing he was evidently referring to the big gray van they had seen from the lookout tree before responding to the sun flashes. Too bad they had not spotted it from the air before parachuting down this time, but no doubt it was parked somewhere well out of sight among the pines.

Flat Nose and Red finally returned with spades, and the crooks began to dig. But after they had gone down more than six feet, it became clear to everyone that the pseudo-grave was empty!

Diablo was furious—especially when he noticed Joe grinning contemptuously at him and the other baffled, sweating crooks. "You punks think you're smart, wasting our time with this foolishness!" Diablo leered. "Well, let me tell you something, my fine young brats—you may be laughing out of the other side of your mouths when I get through with you!"

The Hardys' hands were tied behind them, and the two boys were marched off through the forest to the gang's camp. It was situated near the sandy bank of what Frank guessed must be a deep tidal inlet. Dusk was already falling. In a small clearing behind the gray camper van, two men were cooking steaks on an outdoor grill. One of them had whitish-blond hair and a tanned, seamed face. Joe gasped, and both Hardys recognized him as the crook they had seen at the Pirate's Tavern.

Whitey Waulker!

An unpleasant smile spread over his face as he saw the boys. "So you caught the junior detectives, Diablo? Nice going!" Waulker rasped. "They loused things up for us last night, but something tells me that's the last time they'll interfere with one of your business deals—right?"

"You can count on that, *amigo!*" El Diablo responded in a voice that sent a chill down the boys' spines.

Evidently Waulker had found some way to make contact with the gang after the Hardys had kept him from following the fluorescent blaze-marked trail to the pickup point in the woods. And from the next few remarks, it became obvious that Frank's theory had been correct—Waulker was now waiting for the gang to smuggle him out of the country, beyond the reach of federal law.

Various tools and implements lay scattered about the camp, including a heavy automotive jack. There were also several discarded supply cartons filled with empty cans, bottles, and other trash, as well as two large tires, which looked as though they had been removed from the camper.

Rather than eat in cramped quarters inside the van, the crooks proceeded to wolf down their supper outdoors. Just before they fell to, another man came rushing out to join them. Apparently he had been manning the camper's radio gear.

"The freighter just heaved to offshore, boss!" he told Diablo. "They'll send in their load as soon as it gets dark enough!"

"Good! Tell the skipper I'll be sending the boat back to his ship with an extra load we weren't expecting!" As he spoke, the gang leader shot a vicious look at the Hardy boys, and ended with a menacing chuckle. "Once they've disappeared out of the country, Fenton Hardy will have to do whatever I tell him, if he ever hopes to see his two brats again!"

Frank and Joe looked on hungrily while the gang ate. They had been shoved down into a sitting position among the trash—Frank with his back to the cartons, and Joe leaning against the two big van tires.

Just before being shoved down, Joe had noticed a

shiny glint in the badly worn treads of the top tire. In the circle of light from the camper, his keen eyes had quickly detected the cause—a shard of glass protruding from the tire casing!

By feeling around cautiously behind his back, Joe managed to notch his wrist cords in between the piece of broken glass and the tread. Then he began sawing back and forth.

It was slow, nerve-wracking work, having to start and stop every time he thought one of the crooks might be noticing what he was up to. But finally he felt the last strands of rope beginning to give way.

Nate Grimes was the first of the gang to finish eating. At Diablo's order, he took a pair of night glasses from the camper van and headed seaward on foot along the bank of the inlet to keep watch for the freighter's boat.

Joe sawed frantically, trying to finish cutting the bonds around his wrists. He had no plan except for a desperate hope that once he himself got free, he might be able to pull the piece of glass out of the tire and cut Frank's ropes also.

Suddenly a shout was heard. "Hey, boss. The boat's coming in from the ship!" Grimes hurried back to the camp out of the darkness.

Diablo, who was still chewing on a mouthful of steak, merely waved in response.

Just then, Joe's wrists came free. Desperately, he

tried to think of a way to cut Frank's ropes, too, without being seen.

But as Joe glanced at his brother, he saw Frank grin. There was no need to cut his bonds—he already had them nearly sawed through, using the jagged edge of a tin can in the trash carton!

Diablo belched, wiped the back of his hand across his mouth, and rose to his feet. "Okay, *amigos*," he said. "Get ready to heave those brats in the boat as soon as we unload the goods they're bringing in!"

The other crooks got up, one by one, and turned to look at the Hardys. Red and Flat Nose started toward the two boys.

"Now!" Frank hissed to his brother. Joe groped for a lug wrench lying near the tires, and Frank's fingers closed around the neck of a bottle in the trash carton.

"On your feet, punks!" Red ordered gruffly.

The Hardys rose together, and their hands came out from behind their backs. Each swung hard at the crook nearest him!

20 Treasure Tree

Joe's lug wrench caught Flat Nose on the side of the head, knocking him to the ground! Meanwhile, Frank smashed the bottle against the red-haired thug's temple, and he, too, went down.

"Keep fighting, Joe!" the older Hardy panted. "Maybe the Coast Guard'll spot us!" Both boys realized there was always a chance that the Coast Guard might notice the smugglers' boat and trail them to the cove. It was a slim hope, but enough to inspire the young detectives with an extra measure of courage as they turned back to face their foes.

El Diablo roared with anger when he saw what had happened to two of his men. "Grab those punks!" he shouted.

Nate Grimes and the two other gang members moved fast to obey their chief's command. Whitey Waulker also looked eager to join the fray if more help was needed to subdue the brash youths.

The Hardys fought like wildcats, swinging their makeshift weapons in all directions. Grimes yelped with pain as the lug wrench hit him on the arm, and the gang's cook staggered backward, half stunned by a glancing blow from Frank's second bottle!

The muffled thrum of a boat engine had been growing steadily louder, and presently a heavily laden motor launch thrust out of the darkness to beach itself in the sandy bank of the cove.

"Come on! Give us a hand with these brats!" Diablo yelled and gestured to the two seamen aboard the launch.

With their desperate tactics, Frank and Joe had so far managed to keep their attackers at bay. But now, with El Diablo himself and the two smugglers surrounding them and starting to close in, there seemed little chance that the Hardy boys could go on battling much longer.

Just then fresh voices were heard. Five more figures swarmed into the little clearing. But it quickly became obvious that these were no allies of the gang. Fists flying, they flung themselves on the crooks, grabbing them by the arms or shoulders and swinging them around so that punches could be landed more effectively!

"Dad!" Joe exclaimed joyfully as he caught sight of Fenton Hardy's grim-jawed face. Jack Wayne, Chet, Biff, and Tony were with the big, broad-shouldered detective!

In a few minutes the fight was over. El Diablo tried to draw a weapon with each hand, but a hard right to the jaw by Fenton Hardy sent him sprawling among the trash!

In all, five of the crooks had been knocked off their feet and now remained stunned or cowering on the ground. The others had their hands in the air as the famed private investigator held them covered with Diablo's own gun.

"Find some rope!" Mr. Hardy told his companions.

It was several moments before his sons, winded and panting, could catch their breath enough to speak.

"What a terrific break, you guys turning up when you did!" Frank blurted happily.

"How did you all get here?" Joe added.

Jack Wayne said he had known that dusk would be falling by the time he drove back on the road to a point near where Frank and Joe had parachuted down, and that he would need help to find the fishhook-shaped stream in the gathering darkness.

So he had radioed the young detectives over the CB in Biff's van to meet him at the airfield. Mr. Hardy, who had come to the Pine Barrens to search for El Diablo's gang undercover, had gotten in touch with Jack shortly before he landed, and had promised to be at the airfield as soon as he could.

After they had all met, they had driven as close to the fishhook as they could. Then, using flashlights and lanterns, they had found the stream, and from there the trail of the gang and their captives had been easy to follow to the campsite.

One by one, the crooks were bound and hand-cuffed. Fenton Hardy used the gang's own communications gear inside the camper to summon the New Jersey State Police. The motor launch was found to contain stolen merchandise smuggled in to avoid customs payment or seizure.

A Coast Guard cutter was dispatched to board and take command of the smugglers' ship, which was lying offshore without lights.

"Now a few things become clear in my mind," Frank said while the young detectives and Mr. Hardy were watching the prisoners. "Flat Nose and Red were following you all around Bayport and Shoreham. You were getting in their way. That's why Red fired a dart at you at the concert."

Mr. Hardy nodded. "Unfortunately, they caught on to my disguise."

"Did they steal Mr. Colpitt's map of the Pine Barrens?" Joe asked, telling his father about their visit to the map dealer.

Mr. Hardy shook his head. "I don't think so. The smugglers were not actively looking for the treasure."

"Then it must have been Verrill!" Frank declared.

"Sam told me about Verrill when I last talked to him," Mr. Hardy said. "Verrill's the one who was after the treasure, so I'm sure he wanted the map."

"And I bet he was the one who played Jem Taggart's ghost, too!" Joe put in.

Mr. Hardy smiled. "No. That was me. I wanted to contact you that night, but then I noticed someone prowling around your camp and chased him."

"Verrill again," Frank guessed. "But why'd you walk around the woods in that getup, Dad?"

"It was a good way to scare away snoopers while I was roaming around and watching El Diablo's gang," the detective replied.

Next morning, while Mr. Hardy was briefing the FBI on the outcome of the case, Frank and Joe decided to return to the fishhook site with their buddies. On the way, Joe called Sam Radley on their car radio to verify Ogden Price's story about his cousin.

"I'll check it out for you and call you back as soon as I have the answer," Radley promised.

"Thanks, Sam," Joe replied.

When the boys arrived at their destination, Frank and Joe were eager to try out a new theory about the location of the treasure.

As they moved the shovels they had brought out of the car, Chet asked, "Where do we start digging?"

"First, we have to count off ten paces north," Frank replied.

"I thought you already did that yesterday."

"That was ten paces north from the tip of the fishhook," Joe explained. "This time we'll pace them off from the phony grave."

As Frank did so, the others watched and followed eagerly. To everyone's disappointment, they failed to find another clear-cut clue like the initials *BJ* formed with pebbles. The ten paces merely brought them to a fallen hollow oak tree.

"Now what?" Biff murmured blankly.

"Wait! Look there!" Joe cried suddenly and pointed to a round, wooden structure nailed to the trunk. It was half hidden among the brush where the tree had fallen.

"It's a crow's nest from an old sailing ship, where the lookout used to stand!" Tony Prito said.

185

"Right!" Joe went on excitedly. "Jem Taggart could have gotten it off some old shipwrecked hulk on the beach—or maybe from the very ship they plundered to get the silver. And that could be what he meant by that tricky wording in the letter—*as the crow flies!*"

Frank's pulse began to pound as a thought struck him. Directly below the crow's nest, he had noticed an opening in the hollow tree trunk. And now, as he stooped down and peered up inside the trunk, he saw his hunch confirmed.

"Look what's in the tree!" he exclaimed to the others.

As they joined him and peered inside the trunk, Chet shuddered and gulped, "Jumpin' Jupiter! It's an old skeleton!"

"*Black Jack's* skeleton!" Frank declared.

"And the letter says the silver was buried underneath him!" cried Joe.

"Right! Which means it's somewhere inside the stump!"

Leaping to his feet, Frank turned and began pushing aside the weeds and creepers with which the old hollow tree stump was now densely overgrown. A moment later, as the others gathered around him, he shouted triumphantly, "*Look! There's the treasure!*"

Together, the boys pulled out a heavily loaded

metal chest containing dishes, platters, and other items of silver plate. Though darkened and oxidized by the passage of time, they were much more valuable now than when the Outlaw of the Pine Barrens had cached the treasure inside the hollow oak two centuries earlier—guarded by a dead man!"

The Hardy boys and their friends transported the treasure by car to the State Police post.

On the way, the radio buzzed. It was Sam Radley, confirming that Rupert Price had long ago been cleared of the murder charge against him.

"I'm so glad," Frank said. "Let's tell Rupert as soon as we deliver the silver plate."

The sergeant, who relieved them of the treasure, looked at them admiringly. "You've done a great job," he said with a smile. "By the way, we arrested Verrill this morning. We're holding him until his client decides whether he'll press charges against him for stealing the letter."

"Good," Frank said. "We're glad you rounded him up."

"Your father left a message for you," the sergeant went on. "He'll be in later to talk to Captain Torelli, and he wants you to meet him here."

"Thanks," Joe said. "We have some business to attend to, but it shouldn't take very long."

The boys left the State Police headquarters and drove to Rupert Price's cabin. When they arrived, they noticed a number of cars parked in front, and three men were standing in front of the door.

The boys got out of their sports sedan and walked up to them. "We'd like to speak to Mr. Price," Frank said. "We have a message for him."

"He ain't here," one of the men growled.

Frank and Joe looked at each other. Both boys had the feeling Price was there, but was barricading himself in the house with his friends guarding him against possible arrest!

"Look," Frank said, "it's important that we talk to him. He's a free man and he does not have to hide from the law any longer!"

"I suggest you leave!" one of the Pineys said. "Right now!" He walked toward the boys menacingly, followed by the others. One of them called, "Hey, Charlie, Cleve! We need help!"

Instantly the door opened, and a few more men came out. All advanced toward the boys, looking hostile and ready to fight.

"Get lost!" one commanded.

Joe was angry enough to argue, but Frank pulled his brother by the arm. "No sense starting anything." Turning to the men, he calmly said, "Mr. Price has a decision to make. I realize he doesn't know us, and we can't prove it to him right now, but he's a free man. He can either believe us or go on hiding."

Shrugging, he led the way back toward their car. They were about to pile in, when the door of the cabin opened again and Rupert Price rushed out.

"Frank! Joe! Wait!" he called.

"What—" His friends began objecting all at once, but he waved for them to listen. "It's okay," he said. "I just got a call that those boys were right. I *am* a free man!"

He walked up to the Hardys and began shaking their hands. "Thanks, fellows! I really owe you a great deal, and I apologize for not completely trusting you. But you must understand that I didn't want to go to jail a second time for a crime I never committed!"

"We understand," Frank said. "How did you find out that we were telling the truth?"

"Oh, I know a few fellows around here, and one of them checked with the authorities, not mentioning, of course, that he knew where I was. My friends were ready to take me away and hide me, but I wanted to know, so I insisted that I wait until I got the word."

"I'm glad we could help," Joe said with a grin.

Price gave each of the boys a warm handshake. "Thanks to you, I'm a free man—and a mighty rich one!" he added with a twinkle in his eyes.

"What are you going to do, now that you have all of their money?" Tony asked.

"Take a cruise around the world?" Biff suggested.

"Not on your life!" Rupert replied. "I'll stay right here and open a modern medical clinic for my friends and neighbors, the Pineys!"

"That's wonderful," Frank said, and the others agreed enthusiastically. The men, who had guarded Price so loyally, cheered and applauded. Now that they realized the boys were not enemies but had done Price a great favor, their hostility disappeared and they, too, shook hands with the Hardys and thanked them.

Finally the young detectives got into their car, saying good-bye to Rupert Price and his neighbors. On the way back to the State Police headquarters, both Frank and Joe had a vague feeling of anxiety in the pits of their stomachs. Would this be their last case, or would something else turn up in the future? Something would, called *The Submarine Caper*, and it would require all the sleuthing skill they had.

Suddenly, Frank brightened up. "Hey, I just had a great idea," he said to his friends. "What say we donate the Outlaw's treasure to Rupert Price's cause, fellows?"

The Bayport High gang cheered and agreed.

"That reminds me, I'm famished," Chet Morton put in. "Let's get some burgers and milkshakes before we meet Mr. Hardy. If we don't, I may need medical attention myself!"

The Hardy Boys Mystery Stories
by Franklin W. Dixon

Look out for these thrilling new mysteries in Armada.

The Vanishing Thieves (64)
Frank and Joe's search for a valuable missing coin takes them to California. But they soon realise that they are on the trail of a particularly nasty bunch of crooks . . .

The Submarine Caper (66)
When the plans for a miniature submarine are stolen, the Hardy Boys go in search of the culprits. But high in the Bavarian Alps the young detectives find themselves facing a watery grave . . .

Armada

CAPTAIN ARMADA

HI KIDS!
I'VE GOT THE
POWER TO BRING YOU FUN,
ADVENTURE, AND
EXCITEMENT!

Here are just some of the best-selling titles that Armada has to offer:

☐ **The Whizzkid's Handbook 2** Peter Eldin 95p
☐ **The Vanishing Thieves** Franklin W. Dixon 95p
☐ **14th Armada Ghost Book** Mary Danby 85p
☐ **The Chalet School and Richenda** Elinor M. Brent-Dyer 95p
☐ **The Even More Awful Joke Book** Mary Danby 95p
☐ **Adventure Stories** Enid Blyton 85p
☐ **Biggles Learns to Fly** Captain W. E. Johns 90p
☐ **The Mystery of Horseshoe Canyon** Ann Sheldon 95p
☐ **Mill Green on Stage** Alison Prince 95p
☐ **The Mystery of the Sinister Scarecrow** Alfred Hitchcock 95p
☐ **The Secret of Shadow Ranch** Carolyn Keene 95p

Armadas are available in bookshops and newsagents, but can also be ordered by post.

HOW TO ORDER
ARMADA BOOKS, Cash Sales Dept., GPO Box 29, Douglas, Isle of Man, British Isles. Please send purchase price of book plus postage, as follows:–

  1–4 Books .... 10p per copy
  5 Books or more . . . . no further charge
  25 Books sent post free within U.K.

Overseas Customers: 12p per copy

NAME (Block letters) _____

ADDRESS _____

_____

_____